THE DOG WHO ATE THE VEGETABLE GARDEN & HELPED SAVE THE PLANET

GUERNICA WORLD EDITIONS 20

THE DOG WHO ATE THE VEGETABLE GARDEN & HELPED SAVE THE PLANET

Dorothea Orane Hurley
(A Cheeky Vegan Dog)
&
Margaret Hurley

GUERNICA
World
EDITIONS
TORONTO—BUFFALO—LANCASTER (U.K.)
·2019·

Michael Mirolla, editor
Cover design: Allen Jomoc, Jr.
Interior layout: Jill Ronsley, suneditwrite.com
Cover Illustration: Mary Bergherr
Guernica Editions Inc.
1569 Heritage Way, Oakville, (ON), Canada L6M 2Z7
2250 Military Road, Tonawanda, N.Y. 14150-6000 U.S.A.
www.guernicaeditions.com

Distributors:
University of Toronto Press Distribution,
5201 Dufferin Street, Toronto (ON), Canada M3H 5T8
Gazelle Book Services, White Cross Mills
High Town, Lancaster LA1 4XS U.K.

Second edition.
Printed in Canada.

Legal Deposit—Third Quarter
Library of Congress Catalog Card Number: 2018965158
Library and Archives Canada Cataloguing in Publication
Hurley, Dorothea Orane (Dog), author
The dog who ate the vegetable garden & helped save the planet / Dorothea
Orane Hurley (a cheeky vegan dog) & Margaret Hurley.

(Guernica world editions ; 20)
Issued in print and electronic formats.
ISBN 978-1-77183-448-3 (softcover).--ISBN 978-1-77183-449-0 (EPUB).--
ISBN 978-1-77183-450-6 (Kindle)

1. Animal welfare. 2. Animal rights. 3. Human-animal relationships.
I. Hurley, Margaret, author II. Title. III. Series: Guernica world editions ; 20

HV4708.H87 2019   179'.3   C2018-906606-7
C2018-906607-5

To all life on Earth—
may you be freed from human harm.

Foreword

Humanity's true moral test, its fundamental test (which lies deeply buried from view), consists of its attitude toward those who are at its mercy: animals. And in this respect humankind has suffered a fundamental debacle, a debacle so fundamental that all others stem from it.
  —Milan Kundera (award-winning Czech-born author)

We in the West constitute a society based on violence, oppression, misery, and domination that has led to an ongoing societal trauma from the microscale to the macroscale for all of us—whether we are the oppressors, the oppressed, or both. I see this clearly in how we collectively consume and how we rationalize why it is okay if our products come from a place of suffering, violence, and inequality.
  —A. Breeze Harper (intersectional writer)

My story is about plants. The planet. And animals. About a dog. *Me!* And my humans. Eating only plants. No animals. Yup! And that brings up other stuff. Um hm.

Meg helped me write this book. Makes me a bit testy. Humans "helping." Because they take over. Habit of theirs. Controlling the lives. Of others. That's when they get things wrong! Had to bring her up short. At times.

She's a pain to work with. Says that of me! Too. Thinks she has me pegged. *And* get *this*! Meg puts *her* words. Into *my* mouth. And that's really annoying. But I used what she said. Contrary wise. Here and there to make ALTERNATIVE points. *Yessiree!* When I sniffed *her* INCONSISTENCIES. (Hold on. I'll explain this funny way. Of writing words. Later.) Anyhoo Meg's mother insists we're enmeshed. Whatever that means. "Boundary issues, Dori," Meg says. "Boundary issues."

Once in awhile I had to protest. Do CIVIL DISOBEDIENCE! I'd lie down. Head between my paws. Close my eyes. And ignore her. I'll have you know. So writing took *longer*. Because of my lying around. With my eyes closed. Then we'd get it together.

Tiffs. Stand offs. DISSENT. We made it. To the end. INTER-SPECIES friends. Relating my deeds. And hers. About how she and I try to protect animals. And help the planet. So you can. Too. Understand. When humans eat animals. They damage the world. It's all connected. Harming animals. To how each of you treats different others. To Earth's destruction. And VICE VERSA.

Meg says humans can't tell this story. As well as dogs. Ahem. As well as *this* dog! We live with you. Watch you. Figure you out. A matter of survival. Um hm. We're ETHOLOGISTS! Studying *humanimals*. But a dog can't go it alone. In the literary world. That's where Meg came in.

Every word she wrote down. For me. Is the truth. And that's important. Because if you can't trust a dog. Then who can you trust? Think about it. Who? My human insists I should say *whom*. Not *who*. See! I told you. That stuff slows a dog's creativity. To a *craawl*.

Meg says the hard truths. She brings up. And that I had her include. Might twist*your*knickers. Humph! I think she meant to say: "twist*your*whiskers!" Yup! Hard truths make a dog *radical*! And one more thing. Animals *are* people! Too. Non-human persons entitled to live. Their own lives. To the fullest! Free! From human harm. On a healthy planet.

Wag*wag*wag,
Dorothea Orane

Chapter One
and the Only One

We must always take sides. Neutrality helps the oppressor, never the victim. Silence encourages the tormentor, never the tormented.

—Elie Wiesel (Holocaust survivor, writer,
political activist, Nobel Laureate)

As long as people shed the blood of innocent animals there can be no peace, no liberty, no harmony between people. Slaughter and justice cannot dwell together.

—Isaac Bashevis Singer (Nobel Laureate in Literature)

I am aware that many object to the severity of my language; but is there not cause for severity? I will be as harsh as truth, and as uncompromising as justice. On this subject, I do not wish to think, or to speak, or write with moderation. No! no! Tell a man whose house is on fire to give a moderate alarm; tell him to moderately rescue his wife from the hands of the ravisher; tell the mother to gradually extricate her babe from the fire into which it has fallen; but urge me not to use moderation in a cause like the present. I am in earnest—I will not equivocate—I will not excuse—I will not retreat a single inch—AND I WILL BE HEARD.

—William Lloyd Garrison
(abolitionist and co-founder of *The Liberator*)

Wag*wag*wag. Here I am! *Dori*! I am! I am! *Phisst*! (That's a dog *laugh*. Um hm. Not a sneeze.) Anyhoo. Last summer I ate the whole vegetable garden. I did! With a bit of help. Except for some stalks. Of Brussels sprouts. And the arugula.

It's March now. And this week. I pulled out the last stems. With their little cabbages to chew on. I let Grace and Spike have a go at them. As well. They're Boxers. Too. By the way. But they wear brown coats. With black stripes. White chests and feet. I'd never seen *that* package before.

About vegetables. Ooph! Jumped ahead of myself. I like to jump. *A lot!* Onto humans. Over the garden fence. Onto Spike. Pounce! Then we have a RUMPUS. (I nudged Meg to write like this—R U M P U S—all the fancy words I learn. From her. Um hm. A little VOCABULARY project I thought up. Working on this book. To keep track! Something we dogs do. Track. And keep track.) Anyhoo we have a rumpus. Meg says Wild Things. Wherever *they* are! Have rumpuses. I have *no* idea. What she's talking about. And by the way. Grace is not a dog you want to *jump* on.

My full name is *Dorothea Orane*. Who calls a dog *Dorothea Orane*? Really! A bit much. In my ESTIMATION. For a young white Boxer. Dori suits me better. Meg says she picked Dorothea. Because it sounds closest. To the one I had. Before she and Jack adopted me. Didn't want to confuse a puppy. I guess. No *dog* names. For Grace and Spike. Either. They have *responsible* people kinds of names. Humph! Names of humans. Who read POETRY. And HISTORY. Vote. Buy electricity from sun and wind. Recycle. And play PINOCHLE. Grace Elizabeth and Spike Robert.

My *first* family named me Dorothy. Dot for short. Has a gray-curly-hair-ish sound to it. Anyhoo at five months old. They put me. Onto an airplane. Sent me to Meg and Jack. Who'd just lost a white Boxer girl. Meg still cries. When she tells that story. Grabs my attention. The

4

crying part. So I lick her. I understand. *Lick lick*. Because I miss my sisters. And brothers. *Lick lick*. And my mom and dad. Really really miss them. *Lick lick*. Gentle licks. Not *too* sloppy. Which seem to help Meg. Except when I lick her face. After cleaning. *Under* my tail! Um hm. Well what's left of it.

Madeleine Maud. Maddy for short. The before*me* white Boxer puppy. Meg and Jack say she was drop-dead GORGEOUS. Ooph! Died. Only twelve months old. Had a MASSIVE FATAL CORONARY. On their bed! Jumped. Fell over. Went stiff. Bagging a red ball.

Now Spike and Grace and I are given TAURINE. And CARNITINE. *Every* morning. With peanut butter. So *we* don't have massive fatal coronaries. I had *no*idea puppies' hearts can stop. Just like *that*. Gives me PAUSE. (Wanted to play. With *pause* and *paws*. But decided to hold off. You don't know me well enough. *No*siree. Not yet. Too much GRANDSTANDING. And you won't believe I wrote this book. Um hm.) After Maddy died Meg's daughter Ellie had me flown. *Cargo*! In a crate. To western New York. Then left to wait. In an empty airport building. Very small me. All alone.

In Missouri. Where I was born. I lived with nine brothers and sisters. And a mom. A mostly-black Boxer with *muscles*. Who washed my face. And ears. Every chance she had. And a dad. A brown Boxer. And kind*of*dopey looking. In a loveable way. A very good dad. We had rumpuses. Like I have with Spike.

How I turned out. Looking the way I do. I can't explain. White! With AMBER eyes. And a black nose. And *muscles*. That part I catch. I turn bright pink. When I'm happy and stoked. And someone rubs my stomach. I have one and a half big black spots. On my right ear. Little black spots. Too. Sprinkled all over my body. Meg wants to connect them. With a marker. Maybe they make the *big*picture! She talks about connecting dots. *A lot*! You'll see!

Anyhoo I have a spot above each eye. That goes *up* and *down*. Whenever I'm QUIZZICAL. And the vet. who spayed me. Said I had a *really* big UTERUS. What that has to do. With my looks. I don't know. She charged extra to remove it. Ooph! Nervy. A VIOLATION if you ask me. Which nobody does. About *anything*. Not even *MY* uterus! Um hm. They only ask, "Dori, need to go outside?" And "Want a carrot?" Humph.

Speaking of not asking me. Meg changed my name. Like I said. To *Dorothea Orane*. Lickety-split! As soon as I arrived. One morning in Missouri Dot. That night in New York Dori. Humph. For a couple of days I sniffed around. For a *dori*. Finally caught on. Has a nice ring to it. Though. *Dorothea* means "God's gift." *Orane* means "rising." Funny name from a person. Who doesn't have anything to do. With religion. And God.

Actually I have lots of names. "Puppy" and "Dorito." "Dori*come*." "*Good*Dori." "Dori*no!*" And "*Damnyou*Dori!*" When I chewed the fringe. Off an oriental carpet. That name sent me scrambling. For safety. Under the kitchen table. Because Meg went on a tear. And said, "*DamnyouDori!*" In a loud, *screechy* voice. Grace panted all TREMBLY. I got hiccups. And held my tail down. Well actually. My stump. My long white tail taken. Too. I was five days old. When someone chopped it off. *Threw it away*! Sent to the *dump*! Same for Spike and Grace. Had no choice. After all whatever does a dog have to do. With *her* tail? I ask you. *Grrrrr!* Those EXTENTIONS help us communicate! Folks! We got to keep our ears. At least.

Anyhoo stump-down part worked. Quite well. The storm blew over. Meg rubbed my chest. And said, "I'm sorry Dori. I shouldn't frighten you." Then she held Gracie. Until she stopped shaking.

My new humans took getting used to. Especially when it came to the food they feed us. Which tasted *yecchy*. At first. Grace and Spike inhale their meals. But I had to *work*. At eating smoothies. Of organic purple cabbage and blueberries. (Yup! Meg's NEUROTIC. About giving us organic food!) With kale and ground flax seeds. Hemp. Yams. Nettles. Ginger and turmeric. Just to eat the organic VEGAN KIBBLE underneath. Grace always horned in. And polished off whatever I left. In my bowl. But hunger took me. To the next level. Which Meg calls the "kind diet." Because no one's hurt. No one's CONSUMED. Now I like our mash. Mostly. Got used to it. So Grace doesn't stand a chance. *Nosiree*. Not *any*more!

Grace wants to eat. Eat. Eat. Eat. Her PRIORITY. And she has a *re-ally*slick TECHNIQUE. For getting extra food. Between meals. I've been studying her MANEUVERS. Because resting my chin. On the edge of my dish. And looking PATHETIC doesn't cut it. Been thinking. About using Gracie's act. She puts both front paws. Into her empty bowl. Brings her floppy ears forward. Then upward. Cocks her head *juuust* so. And stands there. Until one of our humans says, "Okaaay, Grace. Here's some food."

But when Meg and Jack read. At the kitchen table. Focused. Style doesn't work. That's when Grace puts one paw. Into her dish. And pushes it. Across the kitchen floor. Makes a *racket*! Then we all get kibble! But just a little. Because they don't want us to become dogs. With *extra*weight. Strains the heart. Ooph! Boxers have CARDIOMYOPATHY. What Maddy had. More than most breeds. So I'm told. Wouldn't know.

It pays to be on Grace's good side. I make sure I lick her face. Often. And wag my tail. *Wildly*! And twist into a knot. Whenever we meet. Let her sniff. Under my tail. After all she knows how to get *the*goods. But sometimes she's SNAPPISH. Maybe her TITANIUM knees hurt. Or maybe she's reminding me I'm number*three*. I make FEINTS. At her. *Woof*! Just to say I won't always be the youngest!

Another thing that I'd never seen. Before I moved in. With Meg and Jack. Spike and Grace. And Maggie*the*cockatiel. Are PORTRAITS. Meg calls them that. She made them. Big paintings of Jack. Of Grace. And Spike. Too. Of Barbara Millicent Roberts. *Barbie* to you! Of *her*kids Ellie and Sam. Who don't look anything like Meg and their dad. They grew up. Before I arrived. And have straight black hair. And eyes shaped like almonds. Maybe she'll paint a big portrait. Of *me*! Someday.

I know about almonds. Because we have them for treats. Two at a time. Spike doesn't like almonds. Hesitates to eat them. We move in. Grace the quickest snatches food. Like a lizard. *Zap*! Snags it. Usually she's the one. Who nabs Spike's almonds. But I kind of let her. Um hm. After all I'm number*three*!

As I said Grace likes food. Um hm. Me too. And loads of other things! So far I've eaten chunks of a rubber ball. (Ooph! Rough output.) Ends of pens and pencils. Reading glasses. A bar of chocolate. *That* sent Meg into a FRIGHT. Chocolate can *kill* dogs! Ooph! Teethed on shoes. Shredded the bedding. In my crate. Chewed up and DIGESTED bits of books. Including *Island of the Blue Dolphins*. *The River Sutra*. *Sistah Vegan*. And five. On Boxers. Used tissues. And a *vegetable* garden.

Now don't get all excited. Just because I mentioned the garden. Again. Doesn't mean I'm ready to talk. About it. Not yet. Even though I consider having eaten the vegetables. A *splendid* feat. I *will* tell you this much. By midsummer those plants looked *really* tempting. You see. I'd become a *vegan*dog! Eating fruits and vegetables. Nuts and grains. Only. Like Meg and Jack. And Grace and Spike. Um hm. Anyhoo the idea of plant-eating dogs winds up humans. Turns them a bit twitchy. When they learn we three don't eat animals and dead EMBRYOS. And SECRETIONS. That's no flesh. No eggs. No dairy! Folks. And no fish. Most insist *dogs are supposed to eat meat!* And that other stuff. Too!

Here it's plants for breakfast. Carrots for treats. Oranges and cabbage leaves. Plants for dinner. Followed by *walks*! *Walks*! I twist myself up. Tight. My nose practically touches my stump. *Walks*! Yipee*yipee*yipee! *Phisst*! Grace bounces straight up and down. As if she has PISTONS. In her legs. Spike's a little less dramatic. Runs back and forth. *Click click. Click click click* go his nails. On the kitchen floor. Faster and faster. *Clickety clickety clickety click*.

Every day Spike and Grace make the neighborhood rounds. With Jack. Meg and I take *long*walks. Usually after dinner. In the evening. Because I chase squirrels. No squirrels to be found then. But so many smells. That require sniffing. Which makes Meg CRANKY. She wants to EXERT herself. I want to DILLYDALLY. And nose about.

Sometimes we have *standoffs*. She growls, "Dori*come*." Root myself. Don't move. She lifts me off the ground. Fifty-nine pounds. Yikes! By my search-and-rescue harness. That no dog can slip! Because I backed out of a harness. Once. Um hm. Meg plops me by her side. "Dori*heel!*" I plunk down my bottom. Lower my head. Lids half-mast. Give her a sidelong eye. My best cut-the-crap attitude. Ordering me around wears thin. When I want to go my own way. At my own speed. And sniff. Anyhoo I win! Meg waits.

Besides somebody's got to poke around. Scout the neighborhood. Stay on top of things. Mr. Rogers would have agreed. With me. He had a neighborhood to mind. His very own! Now he's dead. He ate plants. Too. Like we do! Said he'd never eat anyone with a mother! I have *no* idea. Where that came from. Meg putting words. Into my mouth. Um hm. As I said in the *Foreword*. Habit of hers.

She waits. I sniff. *Nuph nuph nuph.* Dead mouse on the sidewalk. Dog pee on the telephone pole. And hydrant. Sniff deer droppings. In the shadows. Walk a bit. Smell fox. Who crossed the road. Track toads. Whiff of possum. Ooph! Not dead. Walk some more. Sniff rabbit turds. Fast-food wrappers. Recycling bins. When that wears thin. We charge home. For a whirl with Spike. Roll on my back. Spike chews my neck. Shake myself off. *Whup whup whupity whup.* Rush Meg's and Jack's bed. Then we three settle down. Against their legs. And sleep. While they read. And solve crossword puzzles.

Other than an UPHOLSTERED chair. In their office. And Meg's and Jack's bed. N*o one* with four legs is allowed. *Onto* the furniture. In our house. *No one!* But *someone* does climb. *Onto* it. One day as they pulled into our driveway. Meg and Jack saw Grace. Through the large window. Walking. *Across the kitchen table*! Mind you! Another time they caught Grace. Walking. *On a living room table*. They still laugh. About that.

Whenever Meg sees white dog fur. On the couch and chairs. She points her finger. At *me*! With the*look*. Such GALL! I give her my LASER stare. "You know. Lady. I'm not the only one. Around here. With *white* fur!" That's what I think. Um hm. And beam my two *pet*-a-watts glare. At her. That two QUADRILLION watts! Folks. Of burn. What about the other two. With white feet. And chests? Humph.

In front of a big upstairs window sits the chair. The one. Where Spike and Grace and I hang out. Take turns. And watch the neighbors. And our humans at work. They call our chair the *flower*chair. Because it has pink HYDRANGEAS. On blue fabric. Ooph! I keep my mouth shut. About the pink hydrangeas. Anyhoo I have a pretty good view. Resting my head on its back. Shifting my gaze. From side to side. See up and down the whole block. Um hm. If something catches my eye. I stand. With my paws. On the window sill. And grrrowl. That gets me a "Dorioff!"

Lately I've been paying extra attention. To the newcomers who live. Across the street. Well not exactly to *them*. I never see *them*. Which gives *them* a *high*interest factor. *They* moved. Into their house. Late summer. First and last time anyone saw *them*. Now it's March. And *they* still haven't opened their shades. Neighbors nod toward the house. Ask each other, "What's with the shades?" "When will *they* come out?" Meg should try closing our blinds. Um hm. White dog fur. And dust. On the furniture. Wouldn't show.

From the *flower*chair I watch Meg and Jack write. At their computers. And doze. *Tickety tick tick tick tickety tickety tick.* "Shit!" That brings me out of my STUPOR! Meg needs to mind her mouth. I ask you, "How many dogs would let fly such filth?" Not one!

A good place. To shred toys. Too. And think. Sometimes my head draped. Over a bunch of hydrangeas. On an arm. Of the chair. I consider life. As a *vegan*dog. And being *odd*. At least my humans don't make me *obviously* odd. By pinning buttons. Onto my harness. Like the ones Meg wears: *CHICKS DIG VEGANS* and *WEAR YOUR OWN SKIN, NOT OURS*. And *PRO LIFE? DON'T EAT MEAT*. A relief living with people. Who don't make meals. Of my fellow creatures.

Otherwise I'd feel like a kid adopted. By CANNIBALS! I'd become a TRAUMATIZED dog. With ANXIETY ISSUES. And DEPRESSION. Yowza!

My veterinarian eats *murdered* animals. Meg points out. And drinks calves' milk. And she's not the only vet who does! How can someone help animals? Then go home. *Eat* them. And take their babies' food? Reminds her. Meg says. Of Catholic priests. Doing "God's work." Protecting the weak. Helping the needy. Speaking against injustice. And MOLESTING children. By the thousands! *Grrrrrrr!* Twists my stump. Turns my nose upside down. Burns my whiskers. *Wicked!* Um hm.

Meg tells me. That *non*vegans give vegans. A lot of grief. (And the other way around. Too. I tell you!) Meg's mother insists vegans are a CULT. Meg says *vegan* is an ETHIC of NONVIOLENCE and COMPASSION. Another pin she wears reads: *NO ANIMALS WERE HARMED IN FEEDING THIS BODY.* My humans don't eat murdered and raped animals. Not anymore. Yup! They're raped! FORCED IMPREGNATION. Ooph! Don't eat their unborn children. Or drink fluids sucked out of them. Or use anything tested on animals. Or watch animal slaves perform. Like elephants and tigers. And orcas. Stopped. Just like that. Snap! A few years ago. After lots of soul searching.

Meg says you can buy vegan tires. Not only food. Wine. Shoes and clothing. Vegan glue. Vegan medicine! Supplements. Hair dye. Makeup. And vegan tattoos. Yup! Tattoos! I ask you. What pig wants to become tattoo ink? I can't think of one. How many humans know that sows sing. To their piglets? Um hm. Very sensitive creatures. Pigs. And intelligent. They *can* play *video*games! Dare I say? Pigs are *smarter than dogs!* Humph.

In her *Sustainable Living* class Meg's students learn. About farmed animals. Like pigs. That almost all meat and dairy come. From factory farms. They learn why farming animals. (Large *and* small OPERATIONS.) Is the biggest source of Global Warming. In the world. A bigger source than all the machines. That transport people. Ooph! And that animal protein. From flesh and milk can cause CANCER. Ooph! Ooph! Ooph! And DIABETES and ARTHRITIS and DEMENTIA. And ERECTILE DYSFUNCTION. Yup! Listen up guys! Strokes. Heart disease. And COGNITIVE problems. Because when your arteries are clogged. With animal fats. And coated with PLAQUE from animal protein. Less oxygen goes. To your brain. Um hm. You need oxygen to think! Folks. To connect the dots!

Her students read how humans COMMODIFY. And treat billions and trillions. Of animals. One hundred fifty billion land animals. Worldwide. And almost three trillion water animals. Slaughtered *every year*! Let's bring that home. Every year. Nine billion animals killed. Just to feed Americans. That's 975,000 slaughtered every hour. Of every day. Yikes! Bred to be killed for human CONSUMPTION. And corporate profit. And millions and millions more used to make clothes. Used for testing beauty and cleaning products. And for military exercises. Live tortured lives. Endure horrible deaths. Believe me! I've *watched* DOCUMENTARIES! With Meg. About what happens. On factory and dairy farms. In *slaughter* houses! On INDUSTRIAL fishing ships. In science and medical research labs! And breeding FACILITIES. Heard the animals' WRENCHING screams. Seen them thrash. In pain. Makes a dog want to *biiite* humans. And piss piss piss. On their pepperoni and cheese pizzas. On dryer sheets made with fat. From pigs. And chickens. And on their leather shoes. And car seats.

Now I sound all preachy. Like Meg. But boy oh boy Grace and Spike and I are healthier. Eating only plants. Grace and Spike turned eleven. This year. They play around. Like they're five! All bouncy. They don't have yellow teeth and stinky-old-dog breath. And dull fur. Either. *Nosiree! Prance prance prance!*

Meg encourages her parents. To become vegan. Actually she
BROWBEATS them. Has for years! We drive six hours. To their house.
Where she cooks vegan meals. And argues. With her father. Bob.
About eating a whole-foods plant-based diet. And why it's really really *really* important. For their health. For the animals. Who deserve
to live. Who *want* to live. No need to eat them! And for the survival
of the planet. But Bob says he doesn't care to think. About farmed
animals. He enjoys ice cream *every* day! Nancy says she likes the taste
of meat. Yogurt. And cheese. Meg asks them, "Why is your pleasure
more important than their lives?"

Maybe Meg wants Nancy and Bob to act five. Too. They're *an-
cient*. I mean they're practically FOSSILS. In dog years they're older.
Than any dog. Who ever lived. Can you imagine that. Being older.
Than any dog. In history? Meg says there's *her*story. Too. Don't for-
get! And that *his*tory is written by male VICTORS. Not the VANQUISHED.
Whatever. Nancy says she's too old to change.

When we visit them. It's like going to The Mountaintop. Really!
Do you know how much stuff they've crammed. Into their heads.
More than you can fit. In a barn. Um hm. They know as much as
God knows. Maybe more! But Nancy says, "God*only*knows!" A lot!
"God*only*knows what your father's up to!" "God*only*knows when your
sister will arrive!" "God*only*knows why your brother doesn't return
my telephone calls!" I'm pretty sure she does know. Just pretending
she doesn't. To avoid flack. From God. She believes He exists. Um hm.
For being shown up. By a human. And a woman. At that! That's my
THEORY. Anyway. Between them Bob and Nancy dig THERMODYNAMICS.
And ROBERT'S RULES OF ORDER. How to make DOVETAILS. And knit
sweaters. With CABLES. The difference between FURTHER and FARTHER.
You can ask them anything. And they have the answers. Makes a dog
feel stooopid!

But hey! Meg's parents can't smell cancer in humans. Before the
doctors detect it. Or sniff EPILEPTIC seizures. Before they happen.

Nancy and Bob can't keep burglars. Out of the house. By growling and barking. Or jump. As high as the highest branch. On the mulberry tree. In our back yard. Can't wag their tails. (Only have teensy weensy tailbones. Um hm.) Or move their ears forward. And backward! And up and down! *Nosiree!* And her mother and father don't have *ten* nipples. Not even *ten*. Between them!

Spring! So much to do. In the back yard. *Soooo* much. Jobs that require a dog's undivided attention. Someone has to keep an eye. On the place. So I bark. At our neighbor. *Every* time he carries out his trash. He scoots by. Without looking. At *me!* All jumpy. Imagine that! SKEDADDLES. When we three charge the chain-link fence.

Next I check behind the *big*oak. For possums. Run the chipmunks. Off the screen porch. Where they spend the winter. Under the FLAGSTONES. Sniff the compost bin. And tear around. Holding plastic bags. In my teeth. Bags I find. In the bushes. (I kind of like the *ph ph ph ph ph ph ph thrrrrrrr* sound they make. In the wind.) The things I must do. That I plan. In the *flower*chair.

Including my escape. From the backyard! I'd been working. On climbing over the HEDGEROW. That Meg built. Behind our house. Without getting caught. So I could chase a couple of yappy little Shih tzus. I did. Once. Kind of surprised myself. Haven't made it since. The bloke who lives. Behind us. With the yappy Shih tzus STYMIED me. And TORQUED Meg. He tore down her hedgerow! "SOCIOHOPATH," she spat. Then he threw up a cheap crooked stockade fence.

Meg says cheap crooked stockade fences offend her AESTHETIC SENSIBILITIES. Especially when they're painted white. All slap dash. No matter. I have holes. To dig. Saplings to gnaw. Left-out-all-winter toys to find. And flower buds. To remove. Toads and beetles to sniff. And overhead power lines. To MONITOR. I run along. Under them. As squirrels scurry across. Slipping this way. Whoops! And that. Sometimes they fall off. Into our yard! Thud!

Then we have INVASIONS! Zowie! And races to the *big* oak. Squirrels do damage. Eat tulip bulbs. Gnaw trees. Crawl into the walls. Of your house. And chew studs! Roofs. Electrical wires. Ooph! In buildings and cars. They've done 17% of the damage. To the nation's fiber optic network! Imagine that! Squirrels clog downspouts. With nuts. Carry ticks. Drive us dogs wild!

Meg shouts. Disrupts my PURSUITS. "Dori leave the squirrels alone! They have as much right to the yard as you!" Humph. Makes me crazy. When squirrels loll about. Fearless. Checking me out. Flicking their tails. Flick flick. Want to nip them! *Nip nip nip.* They run. In front of moving cars. Causing HAVOC on the roads. Drop acorns. Onto our heads! Terrorize the neighborhood. And Meg and Jack didn't purchase TERRORISM INSURANCE. For our property.

Yup! Really. You *can* buy terrorism insurance. But they checked *NO.* On the application form. Probably because they have a three-point defense. And I'm not talking basketball! Folks. And not Jack. Who's a HOOPSTER. *Nosiree.* I'm talking *three* dogs! Night. And day.

Dogs can conduct HOMELAND SECURITY. Yup! Better than humans. But we'd rather not. Anyhoo we don't require technology. No need for spy cameras. Under bridges. On light poles. In ceilings. On drones. At stop lights. In computers.

No need for human CAPITAL! I'm thinking POMPOUS Transportation Security Administration employees stuffed. Into dark blue uniforms. And Federal Air Marshals carrying pistols. Who use us dogs. To put the *fear* of God. Into humans. Like police. Who harass people of color. With fierce-acting dogs. Too. As if any of that's what *we* want to do. Humph. No need for those Marshals SWAGGERING. Around airports. Posturing with their legs slightly apart. All self-important. Looking as though they've been riding. Since 1850. Across the Great Plains. With the CAVALRY. No need. *Nosiree!*

Pat downs. Unnecessary! And cavity searches. Nope! Ever so nicely. No drama. With our outstanding *noses!* On compact four-legged units. We can *smell* what's under your clothes. Stuffed into your body CAVITIES. And luggage. Under your car. And in its boot. In your shoes. Whether you're wearing clean underwear. Um hm. When we're ordered to protect "your" country. Defend stolen land! How ironic is that? I'd rather sniff scat.

But I'm confusing myself. Talking about *screwy*stuff. Like Homeland Security. When I want to tell you. About meeting Meg and Jack. And Grace and Spike. Maggie*the*cockatiel. Daughter Ellie. Who lives in Utah. And son Sam. Who lives with his dad. And likes to hug me. I didn't meet Ellie Until last summer. When she came home. For a visit. She kissed me. We played tug. *Phisst!* And took *walks*!

Ellie bought me. And gave me to Meg and Jack. After Maddy died. Ooph! Shouldn't mention her name. Starts Meg's crying. All over again. And then she works herself up. Questioning whether it's right to have pets. Over how we OBJECTIFY and commodify animals. Giving them as gifts. Buying and selling them. (Adopted kids. Too!) Separating families. Animal and human. Traumatizing *us*. As if we have no feelings. Don't suffer loss. Have no KINSHIPS. Shipping us far away. All alone. On airplanes. Just to make humans happy. Meet *their* needs! Sooth *their* traumas! But that's not the point. Here. Even though it *is* a *BIG* point!

Anyhoo I was flown. To an airport. In Western New York. Left in an unheated cargo building. In *January*! Not in a warm waiting area. Not even in Baggage Claim. Oh no! FRIGID where I met Meg and Sam. *And* they met me. It works both ways. You know. Successful relationships are 50/50. Including ones with dogs. And *all* creatures. Let me remind you. Usually it's we dogs. Though. Who work hardest. On interspecies relationships. Cats don't care. Just pretend they do! That's my take.

Ooph! Where was I? Right. First when we're little and trying. To understand how to do the living-with-humans act. We're REPRIMANDED. For peeing. And pooping. In the house. For teething. On shoes. Slippers. And chair legs. Whatever's at nose level. Corrected for not knowing how to walk. On a leash. Have you ever heard humans chew out their kind. For yanking and dragging dogs. By their collars.

Damaging *our* ESOPHOGAE. Because *they* haven't learned how to walk. With *us*? Humph!

So we dogs. *Not* humans. Mind you. We *dogs* undergo BEHAVIOR MODIFICATION. Like INDIGENOUS children. Taken from families. Sent to boarding schools. Trained by Christian missionaries to act "proper." By any means necessary. Including violence. For us dogs it's a lot of. Do this! Do that! Bribed. With unhealthy treats. Often forced to wear nasty metal claw collars. That look like INSTRUMENTS. Of torture. And tight collars. With *prongs*! That give us electric jolts. Zzzzzt!

Yup! Our humans command us in *doasIsay* voices to *sit*! *Lie down*! *Off*! And *high five*. (So lame! Like training kids to greet dogs. By sniffing. Under our tails.) To *roll over, no jump, no bark, come, heel*! *Pee*! *Stay*! Whenever *they* want us to. We work on *their* clocks. Not *ours*. At *their* whims. How many people ever put themselves? Into *our* coats? How many? If they did then they might not be so DICTATORIAL. And DOMINEERING. Um hm. They'd be more SOLICITOUS.

Would humans like to be told what to do. Day in. And day out. By us dogs. Bitten every time they disobeyed? They'd have to go. On long hikes. In the countryside. Through fields and woods. Along beaches. Climb mountains. We'd snap at their fingers and heels. When they slowed down. Rain and shine and snow. In heat and cold. Have to wait while we dig and sniff. Play tug and catch. With *us*! For hours on end. Take us for rides. To visit other dogs. Hang around while we swim in the rivers and lakes. In the ocean. And muddy ponds! And chase chipmunks and toads. Run after squirrels. And skunks! Sit and watch life unfold. Sleep wherever. Whenever. Feed us healthy meals. With fresh ingredients. None of this *lazy*stuff. Like greasy kibble. And slop from cans. With animal byproducts. That's *mystery*meat! Folks. Grotty stuff. If only you knew.

There'd be almost no time for them to shop. At malls. For clothes made by abused foreign workers. No time to watch television. *At* least *fifty*hours a week. No time to text. Send selfies. And INANE tweets. Post on Instagram. No time to look. At Kim Kardashian's amazing rear end. And breasts. On the INTERNET. And grill dead animals. Into CARCINOGENS. To whack little white balls around. With metal sticks. On lawns sprayed with poison. They'd have time to think! While we

17

explored and sniffed. And OBSERVED and slept. Now there's an idea! More thinking. About better ways to live. About solutions. For saving our planet. And protecting animals. Being kind. To others. Who are not like them. And about growing Brussels sprouts. Um hm.

Anyhoo after behavior modification. Which comes after the makes-everyone-happy-brand-new-cuddly-puppy stage. When we figure out the love-you lean. And the you-are-the-best-best-person-in-the-world wag. And wiggle. It's downhill. From there. For most dogs. Seems too many humans believe. That if they feed us little hard lumps. Made with GMO corn and soy and wheat and rice with arsenic as the main ingredients. With PUTRID animal parts laced with growth hormones and antibiotics. And who knows what else from rendering plants. Throw a ball a couple of times on weekends and let us out during the day at their convenience (or keep us outside day and night in the cold and heat). Ooph! I need to catch my breath. *Uhuh uhuh uhuh.* And drag us for a few minutes up and down the street roped to them and take us to the vet to have needles stuck into us. Then complain about the cost. (Meg does that! The needle thing. And complain!) Feed us pesticides. That kill fleas and ticks. Then they've met their part. Of the bargain. Ooph! Ooph! Ooph! Sound like *that* woman. Again! On her soapbox. And that's TIRESOME.

Believe me! There's one thing we dogs cannot afford to become. *Tiresome.* Because then we'll be ignored. And lead *miserable lives.* Maybe given away. Dumped! At a shelter to be adopted. By *God*only*knows* what sort of human. Or gassed. Yup! 670,000 dogs. Abandoned and gassed. Every year in the U.S. Alone. So we've got to keep the make-our-people-laugh factor high. And the ecstatic-to-see-you act turned *way up*! For OPTIMUM treatment. And that takes *significant* effort! Folks. And *craft*! And requires HUMILIATING ourselves. Oh I wish Jack would stop me. When I go all preachy. Like you know who! Or is it *whom*? Humph.

So there I was. Sitting in my dog crate. Shivering. In an empty airport cargo building. Peering out. Wondering. What exactly? I can't remember. Probably something like, 'When can I go home. Where it's warm. To my brothers and sisters? And pounce on my dad? And lick my mom. And she lick me?' There I was. Knot in my stomach. Waiting. When two *eager* humans rushed in. A woman with short brown hair. And a young man. With straight black hair. And those almond eyes I told you about.

The woman skooched down. Peered into my crate. Opened the door. "Hi Puppy!" I moved my tail. Back and forth. Just a little. Mind you. Wag*wag*. Stood up. And gave her a *tiny*lick. On the nose. Gently tried out the lick-as-greeting gig. To scc how she'd react. She pulled me. Into her arms. And kissed me. On my head. Suddenly I felt homesick. And brokenhearted. But no one noticed.

"Here, Sam. Want her?" she asked. He held me. Gently. "Everything will be all right, Mom." I had *no*idea why he said that. Sounded *hopeful*. Though. Seemed something had happened. A sad and *fear*some thing. Perhaps? But that was more than this puppy. Without her furry family. And confused. Could understand. Who'd spent five care-*free* months. Romping with her brothers and sisters. In the fields of Missouri. Now alone. In the arms of strangers. Me. A puppy. Who didn't know she'd been sold.

"What kind of dog is that?" people ask Meg and Jack. When we walk. Through the neighborhood. What do they mean, 'What kind of dog is *that*?' I'm a Boxer! "She's a Boxer," my humans say. "Oh," some reply, "Never seen a white Boxer." A bit uppity Meg says, "Used to be most were killed. And some still are." Often she shocks to make her *points*. Especially when it comes to how humans treat animals. One another. And the planet. And how all that connects. Kind of leashed together. Each to the other. And she *bones up*. Ooph! Not a vegan expression! On facts. Lots of facts. For making her cases.

I'm glad Meg and Jack adopt white Boxers. I'm glad my first human family didn't have my white sister and me put to "sleep." Stupid EUPHEMISM for *murder*. My sister has a vegan name! Pepper. Or was her name changed? Too. Has little black spots. Like mine. Some people took her away. Just like that. She smelled of rain. We slept side by side. My head on her neck. In our furry pile. Suddenly gone. I miss her. Feel hollow. And achy. When I remember Pepper. My mom and dad. And the other puppies. They lost me. And I lost them. Do *you* understand?

Meg says twenty-five percent of Boxers are born white. Dog shows don't allow white Boxers. Humph. But that's okay. With me. I wouldn't want to be trained. To be OBEDIENT. I'd have to *shut up*! Be handled and fluffed. Perfumed. Trotted around. In front of judges. Who'd never appreciate my INSOUCIANCE. To win COMPLIANCE competitions. Humph!

Anyhoo breeders require new owners. Hate those words. *Breeders* and *owners*. Sounds like the master-slave arrangement. Make our new *companions* sign papers. Promising *not* to breed white Boxers. As if we're some kind of PLAGUE. And even if we were bred. It wouldn't be our choice. Not every female dog wants to submit. To random horny males. *Grrrrr!* Like I said. Some breeders still kill white Boxers. When they're born. Believe they're less healthy. But that's a MYTH! Tell me who could *kill* white Boxer puppies?

"For that matter what screwy ideas. What desperation. What fear. What anger and hatred drive a human to harm and kill any animal?" Meg asks aloud. To no one in particular. Because I'm not interested. In listening to more. Of what she has to say. But then. When she's fiery. I get caught up. In her frustration. And outrage. In her self-RECRIMINATION. That part's interesting! Um hm. So here it is. Coming your way. Straight from the soapbox. Like it. Or not!

Kind of long-winded. With guilt? Yup! I sniff *guilty*shame. Smells just a bit like rotten eggs. Meg asks, "What kind of human imprisons animals. In filthy stockyards. Knee-deep in urine and manure? In aquariums. In MURKY water to swim in circles? Grinds up 'useless' male chicks, alive. Crams animals into crates and cages, where they can't turn around and can't lie down. Can't nurse their young, while waiting to be killed for meat? Beats them with sledge-hammers. And shoves electric prods up their anuses to drive them to slaughter? Kicks them, slams them against walls and concrete floors, bashes them with cement blocks, when they're too weak to move? Sticks hooks into their mouths and brains. Drags them out of the water, drowning them, slowly, in air, flipping and flopping in anguish. Takes a knife to their throats. Cuts off their heads?" Meg says, "Most humans cannot do this to animals." But Meg did. Chopped off a chicken's head. And gutted fish. For food. Drove pigs to a slaughterhouse. Then shut the murder. Out of her mind. Now she's ashamed to tears. Tormented. Haunted. Wishes she hadn't. Most cannot do that themselves. So they practice being HEEDLESS. Refuse to imagine the horror. Pay others to kill. Out of sight. For food and clothing. And car seats. Medicine. Cosmetics. Decorations. Handbags. Amusement. Tattoos. And crayons. Yup. Crayons are made with animal fat! Folks. Um hm.

"What human traps?" Meg tries to understand. I can't. "Forcing animals to endure terror and unbearable pain for hours on end. Sometimes for days. And to escape they chew off their own paws. And legs caught in the metal teeth. And for what? What kind of human baits animals with food, then shoots them and hooks them like online predators? Who uses electric shock and sharp prods, so, enslaved, depressed, joyless, they *will* amuse the circus and water park crowds?" Makes this dog want to *vomit*!

"People who hurt, hurt others," Meg explains. Perhaps to herself? Is that what it takes to shoot bolts. Into animals' brains. Then gut them alive? Screw wires. Into their skulls. Stand by while they WRITHE. Recording their experiments? Test painful products on them? Until they die. Skin animals alive for their fur? Burn off their beaks. So they can't peck the other hens. Squeezed together? Pull out their teeth. Grind them down. To nerve endings. Without anesthesia. So they can't bite the others. In too-crowded pens. Where they go mad? Force mash down their throats. To enlarge their livers. To make foie gras? Gun down animals for "sport?" For military target practice. And use them. For military medical training. Cutting off legs. Burning flesh. Slicing open stomachs. To expose organs. Without blocking the pain? Shackle them. Then suck out their bile and blood. Milk. Semen. Urine for women's estrogen therapy? Ooph! *Uhuh uhuh uhuh uhuh.* I need to *calm down!* Breathe. Iiinn. Breathe. Ouut. Iiinn. Ouut. "All barbarity that myths, habits, machismo, traditions, tastes and vanity demand. That ignorance and insecurity and self-deception assure," says Meg.

Meg and Jack talk. About how really really sick they felt filled. With sickening sorrow. When they grasped the suffering. Meg INFLICTED. With her own hands. And the misery and death they purchased. "What kind of humans are we?" They asked each other. "If we eat meat and dairy? Fish and eggs? Especially when no need exists. When there's *no* sound argument that animal-based foods are necessary for wellbeing." No organization. According to my humans. In the world says eating only plants is unhealthy. "Not even the Academy of Nutrition and Dietetics. A very conservative group," says Meg. Um hm. Not convinced? Check it out. (Just make sure. I'm told to remind you. That the meat and dairy and poultry and fishing industries didn't sponsor the research you read!)

"What do we value?" asked Meg and Jack. "If we wear leather. Wool. Fur. And feathers. Keep animals as pets? For *our* pleasure!" (Now there's a *good* one!) They thought about all that. Wondered what took them so long to see. The lives they denied others. Ooph! Ooph! Ooph! Kind of went into shock. Kicked themselves. Ooph! Really kicked themselves. When they realized the unnecessary and horrific BRUTALITY their diets. And vanity caused animals. Day in and day out. Year after year. For decades. "Why didn't we question any of this?" asks Meg. Still distressed. "Why didn't I?"

She found a quote from vegan philosopher Arthur Schopenhauer. Says it like it is. "He who is cruel to animals cannot be a good man." They GRAPPLED with the fact. That even if you don't hurt others. Yourself. But have the brutal work done. For you. Then *you* are COMPLICIT. "We were guilty by association," said Jack who's an attorney. All their lives. They had been ACCOMPLICES. In cruelty. "Either way. Shoot the gun, yourself. Or pay someone else to do it. You're guilty of a crime," Jack says. "That's Criminal Law 101. Unless you have no choice. Live in a food desert. Are forced to eat prison meals. And public-school free and reduced government breakfasts and lunches. Outcomes of racist and classist laws and policies," Jack reminds Meg. "That profit the meat and dairy industries."

This *is* big. Think about it. Folks. Humanity fed and clothed. Off the suffering and murder. Of your fellow creatures. Your animal kin! And mine. Where's compassion in that? Especially in this day and age? When this horror is not necessary. Not not *not*! Breeding SENTIENT beings. For slaughter. Eating them. And their eggs and fluids. Eighty percent of America's crops. Turned into dead animals. *Not* necessary for OPTIMUM health. Ooph! Ooph! Ooph!

This myth. That people must eat animals is MONSTEROUS. Makes it okay to deny billions and trillions. Of SENTIENT beings their right. To life. Free from human harm. To bring them into this world to betray them. Land and water animals plan. Give and receive joy. Love. Remember. Grieve. Nurture their young. Protect one another. Create. Solve problems. Live in communities. Form nations. Have families And friends. Want full natural lives. Without suffering. At the hands of humans. I do. And our purposes have nothing to do. With *you*! With any human! Really!

Ask Alice! Meg told Jack. About her. She writes books. Too! One of her stories made Meg cry. Something about purple. Anyway Alice wrote a *very*important truth. "Animals were not put on Earth for the purposes of humans any more than Blacks are here for the purposes of Whites and women for men." I want to ask Alice how she can believe that. And not be vegan! And something about a Jefferson airplane. About asking Alice. "When she's ten feet tall."

Meg says that's a song. That has nothing to do. With the writing Alice. About not fitting in. Being disruptive. Standing up for what's right! Not fighting a war. In Vietnam. What is Vietnam? And what kind of an airplane is a Jefferson? I don't get it. Don't get a lot. Of what Meg talks about. Frustrates me. No end. Like dog collars. Rabies shots. Losing my uterus and tail. Wondering about my dog family. And walks hitched to a human. Humph.

Anyhoo why can't Meg tell you this stuff. *Herself*? Hmm? Why must I do the hard work? Meg making me say things. That people don't want to hear. Making me quote her. Using me. Because I'm a PERT puppy. To rain. On your parade. Crinkles my whiskers. That's animal abuse. Too! You know. Not my purpose to let her. Off the hook. (Ooph! Not a vegan expression!) I think she wants me to be her poster pet. For veganism. Humph. Humph. Humph. And *HUMPH*!

But somebody must speak. For us. The animals. Put our reality in plain sight. From where we stand. And perch. Swim. Cling. Crawl. Fly. Slither and hop. Might as well be a dog. Got to stick my nose into this stinking mess. That humans created. By eating animals. And their secretions. Sink my teeth in. Chew on it. Spit out the truth. Ooph! Ooph! Ooph! You can't see me. Wagging my tail. Furiously! Now that I've told you this I-don't-want-to-hear-it stuff. Wag*wag*wag. Wag*wag*wag. If I could I'd lick you. Too. Wag*wag*! Make you feel all special. Lick lick lick. I'm sure that what I've said. About humans harming and killing animals. Has you *vexed*. Feeling judged. And pissy.

Not to worry. You *can* become *more* compassionate. More peaceful. By not eating creatures. Not anything that comes out of them. Either. And that includes those. Who live. In the water. Wag*wag*wag. *Wag*wag. And dairy products. I mean do you know what happens. To dairy cows? (And goats and sheep)? They're impregnated. Meg cuts to the chase. Says it's *rape*. Rammed into contraptions called *rape racks*! Humph. Should be called rape *wracks*! Then she winds up. Sets in. I'm just passing it along.

Again and again. Farmers stick their hands deep. Into the cows' vaginas. Up to their elbows. And squirt semen. Into them. Collected by electric shocks. To the bulls. ELECTRO EJACULATION. That would be called "torture." Folks. If it were done to humans. To keep the cows LACTATING. Impregnated over and over. So they have babies. One after another. And make more and more milk. ESSENTIAL NUTRIENTS stolen. From their calves. Who are taken from their mothers. The day they are born. So people can eat dairy products. Not meant for them. After a few years the cows' uteruses fall out. From too many pregnancies. And drag. On the ground.

Young mother cows *worn*down. Sucked dry by machines. Every day. For hours. *Suck. Suck. Suck.* Their teats infected. Filled with puss. *Suck. Suck. Suck.* And sore. Their fly-swatting tails chopped off. To make it easier. For farmers to attach the milking machines. *Suck. Suck. Suck.* Overwhelmed. With *never*ending grief. From having their newborns kidnapped. Crying out to them. For weeks. And weeks. After each birth. After a few years. Of *constant* agony. Humans shoot bolts into their brains. And shackle the stunned cows. In chains.

Hung from the ceiling. By their hind legs. Sliced open alive. Choking on their blood. Gushing from their throats. Kicking and twisting. Ground into hamburger. Their female babies. Well you get it. The same fate. Serial rape and slaughter! Again and again! Their baby boys killed. After a few months. Of their own hell. Ooph! Ooph! Ooph! Don't think this TIRADE is over. Folks. There's more!

Bull calves murdered. At sixteen weeks. Suffer in tiny stalls. Can't move. Can't lie down. And have no water to drink. MALNOURISHED they become ANEMIC. Because humans like to eat pale and soft sick babies' flesh. Called *veal*. Clever word. No need to think. About eating another mother's tortured child. Because humans have forgotten. *Veal* means *little*calf.

On the way to slaughter the baby boys. Who miss their mothers so. Desperate for milk. Try to suckle the fingers. Of their killers. Or too weak to move they're thrown. Into dead piles. Starved. Stripped. For calfskin clothing. Like the skins of Jews. Meg points out. Used by the Nazis. For lampshades.

And *please*. Pretty pretty*please* with *lick*licks. For all animals' sakes. Don't buy leather. Fur. Wool. No pillows and comforters. And coats. Filled with feathers. And down. Yanked from geese and ducks *squawking* in ANGUISH. Nothing made with fur stripped. From live Angora rabbits and foxes. Dogs. Cats. And other furry creatures. Left to die bloody and skinned. *Pleeease*. And buy cruelty-free products. Look for soaps and lotions. And cosmetics. With a drawing. Of the little leaping bunny. On their containers. No products made with animal parts and secretions. No goat's milk soap. Either. No products with beeswax. No Retin A for your skin. It's made from the cartilage.

Of dead cows. And boycott organizations that force animals. To amuse humans. Ooph! *Please*. This is all too much. For a puppy. To think about. Who only wants to curl up. In the *flower*chair. Snooze on the pink hydrangeas. And forget everything I ever told you.

This week Meg and I drove to Vermont to visit Nancy and Bob. And Sophie*the*dog and Willie*the*cat. Sophie and I bounce around. Tumble and chase each other. Nancy and Bob don't like our high JINKS. Nancy's lips pinch. Sophie seems lonely. Bob orders, "*Sophieliedown*." Otherwise he mostly ignores her. Always Sophie waits. For Nancy's attention. And Meg's brother James to play. With her. When he visits. No one walks her. Never have. Now she's too old to hike down the lane. Makes my ears droop. Flattens my stump.

A long ride. I looked out the window. Slept. And ate my organic vegan treats. Which I get. With my high-pitched whine. *Eeeeeeeunh*. That *really* annoys Meg. I watched MIGRATING geese fly. In Vs. Above Montezuma National Wildlife Refuge. Deer grazing in fields. And wild turkeys. Who eat ticks.

More and more ticks. Every year. Meg says the planet's heating up. Ever so quickly. Winters aren't as cold. Now the ticks don't die off. As much. Lots of ticks. In Vermont. This year. They killed seventy-five percent. Of the baby moose. My humans don't use flea and tick products. On us. Because they're *pesticides*! Yikes! Meg sprays us with cedar oil. Rubs food-grade DIATOMACEOUS earth. Into our fur. Kills fleas. Ooph! A tough choice. For someone who doesn't want to kill creatures. And picks off ticks.

I stared at Price Chopper and Wegmans and Sysco trucks. With huge photographs. Of red meat. Thick slabs. And semis carrying dairy products. Like Hood. Bet Meg will write. To those companies. About their EXPLOITATION. Of helpless creatures. "Please do not use images of *murdered* animal parts on your trucks. And pictures. Of white animal fluids. Please don't use cruelty for profit."

As for me I want truth. In advertising. Like the bumper sticker that reads: *EVERY PIECE OF MEAT BEGINS WITH AN ANIMAL BEGGING FOR HER AND HIS LIFE.* I want different pictures and words. Show reality. On those trucks. A sheep and her lamb. A cow and her calf. A Sow and her piglets. A chicken and her chicks. A goat and her kid. A fish and a lobster and a shrimp. With their young. Next to chunks of *their* flesh. Dead embryos. In egg shells. And glasses of *their* splashy milk. On tankers and containers. With the words: "If you eat meat and dairy, you pay others to steal my baby. Take my mother from me. My brother. Sister. My father. Torture her. Torture him. Rape them. Suck us dry. Murder us. Enjoy our flesh! Enjoy *our* babies' food!" Like the large mobile signs. In New York City. That showed b*eautiful* women. Meg told Jack about them. Wearing expensive *fur*coats. Next to images. Of *bloody* animal carcasses. Stripped. Of their skins. Alive? (The fur industry says it doesn't do that. But do PROFITEERS tell the truth? Humph.) For those coats. Frizzles my whiskers. Sears my ears. Turns my toenails around and upside down. *Grrrrr*!

We followed the Mohawk River. Could almost walk. From bank to bank. Because of the drought. Through the Leather Stocking District. Ooph! *Leather*. We raced the trains. Drove across the pale blue bridge. High. Over the Hudson Valley. Made me QUEASY. But soon after we turned north. Into PRISTINE Vermont. Where Meg grew up. I sensed her relax.

Vermont doesn't look like Missouri. Not like Western New York. Either. So much green. In Vermont. Rocks. Pink grass. Really! Pink grass! And mountains. No billboards. Beside the highway. Along the Connecticut River. No litter. And a state capital. With *no* McDonalds. The only one in the country. With *no* McDonalds. Meg says so. Um hm.

And there are villages and towns. Where people have meetings. Before they vote. Bob said the Frenchman de Tocqueville wrote. About New England's town meetings. As the world's truest form. Of DEMOCRATIC GOVERNMENT. Maybe so. But that means nothing. To me. I want to know. Can dogs go. To them? Sniff around! *Nuph nuph nuph.* Check out humans' behinds. Poking through backs. Of folding chairs! Meg says Vermonters are CUSSED. I agree. If they're *any*thing like Meg. And Bob and Nancy. Imagine all those cussed Vermonters. Together! DISPUTING! Maybe dogs would smooth things over a bit? You think?

Meg grew up. In a town. Where everyone knows everyone. Has a general store. With a name that Jack thought was Polish. The first time Meg told him the name. Of the store. He heard *Danowitz*. Now they call Dan & Whit's. ("Grammatical error," says Meg. Um hm.) "The Danowitz."

Dogs sit outside The Danowitz. And wait. For their people to buy maple syrup and nails. Mixing bowls. Flowers and wine. Bandanas. And leather cow collars. Yowza! Imagine that! Wearing a collar. Made from your relative's skin. (My nylon lemon yellow collar has raspberry pink polka dots. It does! *Spiffy.*) And big metal scoops and sushi. And the *Valley News*. With articles about hunting. And dairy farms. And fishing. That give Meg a fit. Ooph! The Danowitz is something else. Maybe someday they'll let dogs go. Inside! I'd sniff the nail bins. And check out the garden tools. And seeds. And pee. On the hunting gear! And fishing poles. Make the whole lot stink! And on the meat and dairy cases! Rust them *out*!

Until he met Meg. Jack had never been. To Vermont. Same as *me*! Ooph! I can hear her now. Correcting students. "'Me' is the OBJECT OF A PREPOSITION. Use *I* as the subject. Same as *I.*" And she wouldn't stop there! Oh no! "*I* is a NOMINATIVE SINGULAR PRONOUN." Yup! English teachers can be IRKSOME. But Meg says she isn't a teacher. Nooo! Says she's a SUBVERSIVE. Who teaches. What do I care? No school for me! *Phisst*! *Prance prance prance!*

As we drove into town Meg said, "That's my elementary school." Where she punched a mean girl. During recess. In fifth-grade science class she watched a MONARCH BUTTERFLY appear. From a pale-green

CHRYSALIS. With gold dots. Pointed out the town hall. Where she and her brother James shot hoops. (Ever notice humans' *violent* language? Shooting. Animals. Photographs. Hoops. Each other. Wads. Daggers. The breeze. Their mouths off. Giving things a shot. Hot shot.) Anyhoo where they played basketball. During the summers. We passed the church. With the Paul Revere bell. Where she married. Her first husband. Long ago. He went to the same institute of TECHNOLOGY as Bob. But he's not cussed. Because he's from California.

Passed her family's big old house. On Main Street. Up and down the sidewalk. She and her friends walked. In togas. Made from *bed*-sheets. Across from The Danowitz. Where she saw a man. Push Fiona their German Shepherd. Into his car. In the general store's parking lot. Meg screamed, "Stop him!" And Nancy did! Marched right over there. Grabbed the dog. Blasted the thief. A real tongue lashing. No town police back then. Being cussed comes in handy.

Lots of dust-ups and MISHAPS. And projects. At their big old house. Meg's youngest brother Charlie stuck his sword. Through an etched glass panel. By the front door. When he was little. And he shot the TV with his BB gun. Watching *Gunsmoke*. On the sly. Best of all she and her brother James threw tomatoes. Over the backyard fence. At the neighbors' teenage son. Who'd held Meg's head down. In a snow bank. After school.

In the guestroom bathtub. Meg soaked SAPLINGS. For weeks. To make a Halloween costume. A sixteen-foot dragon. Bet that made Nancy's lips go all thin. And tight. Having the tub occupied by a PROTO dragon. Meg bent the wet branches. And lashed them. Together. Same as the Boy Scouts.

She tried to join the Boy Scouts. Three times. She did. Dreamed of adventures. Canoeing rivers. Camping in snow. Building fires. And peeing in the woods. Didn't want to weave nylon potholders! And bake cookies. With Girl Scouts. Wearing a green dress.

But the boys voted *NO!* Three times *NO!* So she made a dragon. Bob was the scout master. He taught her how to use saplings. To make the frame. For the fabric skin. An old sheet she painted JADE.

With yellow spots. And big white teeth. Imagine that! Sat back. On my haunches. When I heard this story. No dog *ever* BEGAT a dragon! "Begat." Like that? Kind of snappy sounding!

From the age of eight Meg lived. In the Main Street house. With three dogs. Two cats. And a Quarter Horse. Who pulled down the side porch! Where she and her friends acted. In *Heavens Blue Blood*. The five SIBLINGS had gerbils. Too. Hamsters. Rabbits and guinea pigs. Who starved. Because the kids were lazy. Didn't feed them. Ooph! Ooph! Ooph! Meg still struggles. With hot shame. And she wonders why. Her parents didn't step in. And protect their helpless pets. Who suffered long slow deaths. After eating their young. In the dark damp basement. And barn. Where they suffered and PERISHED.

Before the guinea pigs died. And still of interest. Meg dressed them. In doll clothes. For rides. In an old wicker carriage. A couple of parakeets. Named Verdi and Toscanini. Lived in their kitchen. And a rescued baby raccoon. Who jumped. Into the baked custard. Cooling on the stove top. Nancy never told Bob. And served the dessert. To his mother! Um hm. Who informed my human she wouldn't amount to much. Guess Meg's grandmother hadn't seen the dragon!

April's here! Jack's been studying seed catalogues. And I want to know will those two ever plant the garden? This afternoon I was really focused. On vegetables. Sniffing around the plot. When Meg came home. From school. *Upset!* Like LIVID. A teacher and a student had killed a mouse. The teacher bashed her. And bashed her. And *bashed* her. *Bunk bunk bunk*! With the big blue plastic recycling bin. *Bunk bunk bunk. Bunk!* Meg witnessed the killing. "*Stop! STOP!*" she yelled. "*Noooo!*" That's when the smiling boy stomped. On the small shaking and broken body. And smashed her skull.

The little gray field mouse. In the classroom. Running running running. From the screaming teenagers. And the bashing bashing *bashing* teacher. And the stomping student. Smiling pleased as Punch whacking Judy. He picked up her little crushed body. With a paper towel. And threw it. Into the trash. With half eaten slices. Of cold greasy pizza. Wads of chewed blue gum. Snotty tissues. And donut boxes. He SMIRKED. *Smirked!* The little mouse wanted only crumbs. Of food. Left by the class. That's all. She was hungry. Probably. And maybe cold.

Sitting together. On the edge of the bed. Meg told me this. Her arm around my shoulders. She asked, "Dori, what did the teacher teach his students today? He taught them to harm those who are defenseless. And vulnerable. He taught them to kill. To destroy those who are different. Who scare you. And dispose of those who disturb your world. He taught them to ignore compassion when it requires effort and restraint. He taught *racism!*"

Then she hugged me. And added, "The teacher ignored the deadly lessons of the Klan. Pol Pot. Argentina's genocidal president Bignone. And Hitler. The irony, Dori, he's African-American. His ancestors were slaves. He goes to church. Fought in Vietnam. And he teaches history. *History!* He didn't teach his students what Harriet Beecher Stowe said the 'best people have always done. Take the side of the weak. Against the strong.' Why?"

Meg went on, "He would probably defend himself: 'For God's sake woman, *IT* was only a mouse.'" Strange she didn't say anything. About how humans call animals *IT* and *THAT*. Objectify them. Instead of *she*. Or *he*. *Who*. Or *whom*. Or any other pronoun. That refers. To a sentient being. Said nothing about how *IT* refers. To a thing. And 'diminishes the mouse's significance.' She didn't point out. Either. That by thinking. Of animals as things it's easier to disregard their feelings. Needs. And suffering. Ooph! Meg sighed, "Maybe the mouse had babies, who will die, now." And "I have a headache." As for me ... I don't know what God had to do. With any of that.

Today Meg and Jack protested puppy mills. They didn't take me. And Spike and Grace. The organizers emailed, "Don't bring dogs." Meg and Jack said ACTIVISTS held signs. Some read: *YOUR PET STORE PUPPY'S MOM IS DYING IN A PUPPY MILL*. And *FOR EVERY PUPPY YOU BUY, A SHELTER DOG DIES*. And *ADOPT DON'T SHOP*. So get this. My humans shopped for *me*! On line. Um hm. But that was before they connected the dots. And bought Boxers from breeders.

Anyhoo Meg and Jack protest stores that sell fur. And a parade in Vermont. With farmers and farm kids. Dragging fearful dairy calves. Down the street. And now you know what happens. To them! Protest animal circuses. And pig scrambles at county fairs. Where terrified piglets chased by humans. *Scream*. For their mothers. Then thrown into sacks are tied up. After they're caught. Given to the winners to do whatever they want. With the piglets. They protest circuses with animals. And water parks that use sea mammals. Because they are beaten. Too. Shocked and abused. Kept in too-small tanks. Forcibly bred. Trained. Enslaved. Live sad. And depressed EXISTENCES.

I wish I could have gone with them. And sat in the sun. And wagged my stump. At the protestors. Who love dogs. And who probably eat meat and dairy. Because they haven't thought things through. Yet. I would sniff them. While they oohed and awed, "She's so cute." I think I should have gone. And made a *point*. Too. Um hm. How in this world. What happens to us animals is less important. Than how much money can be made. By humans and corporations using *us*. Yup! My sign would have read: *ANIMALS AREN'T FOR PROFITS*.

Have you held the word *DOG* up to a mirror. Go ahead. Try it. What do you see? Another way of considering us! You know we don't kill*kill*kill millions. Of our own kind. And billions*billions*billions and trillions. Of other species. Every year. And PLUNDER and PILLAGE and POLLUTE the planet. Only one species does that. Um hm. As for dogs. We love.

And forgive. Now tell me. Who are the superior beings? Humans or dogs? Go ahead. You can do it! Deeeep breath. Say CANINES!

Just because humans invented paper clips and Facebook and fighter jets and Google and *smart*phones and pesticides and forced-animal breeding and GMOs and highly-processed junk foods and self-driving cars and Bohemian Grove and assault rifles and silicone breast implants. For humans. *And* show cows! Yup! And silicone testicles for neutered dogs. Ooph! And voter suppression. Water boarding and factory farms and *slaughter*houses and hydrogen bombs and hydro fracking and drones and legalized slavery in for-profit prisons and Mar-A-Lago and reality TV. Does that make them superior? Is all that superior. To dogs' love. And forgiveness?

We protect. And tend humans. *Okaaay*. So we scare the bejesus. Out of squirrels. And cats. Skunks. Woodchucks. And rabbits. Anyhoo we use what we need. And no more. Only leave compostable NUTRIENT-RICH materials. On the ground. That BIODEGRADE and benefit nature. We reduce humans' stress. Help the most-destructive *predators*. On the planet relax. Bring them joy. How much more godly can a species be? Think about *that*. As you hold the word *DOG*. Up to a mirror.

Spring break. We drove to Vermont today. To visit Nancy and Bob. Again. Meg brought vegan peanut-butter dog biscuits. In the shape of *bones*. For me. Explain that. Please. Why not in the shape. Of *peanuts*? Um hm. We dogs are not *dimwits*. We know *vegan* treats have *no* meat in them. So why try to trick us. With bone shapes. Into thinking they do?

We moved along. At a clip. Fluffy white clouds. Dog-dish blue sky. Sun. Silence. No radio. No music. Meg ignored me. Had that deep-in-thought blank look. I rested my chin on the back of the seat. And watched the world. In reverse. People in cars pointed. To me. And smiled. Saw a dead deer. In the breakdown lane. Her head thrown back. Rushing traffic ruffled the white fur. Under her tail. Hawk flew overhead. With a mouse. In the fast lane lay a squashed skunk. Dead woodchucks. We've seen a raccoon. With half her body torn away. Mouth pulled back. In agony. Dead dogs. Dead opossums. A small sad red fox. Sitting in the road. Beside her smashed mate. DEVASTATED. With a "what-do-I-do-now look" on her face. Passed a cow in a trailer. She called, "*Mooooo. Mooooooooo.*" Heard Meg's breath catch. A pained squeak. The cow called again. *Mooooooooo.* Her eyes wide. With fright. My ears drooped. Made me weak in the knees. Ached. Could this be the feeling. Of woe?

Like the tracks that parallel them. Interstate highways are ani-mal *die*ways. Vehicles hit and kill us. Trucks drive us. To our deaths. Beside the highways. Trains carry animals. Crammed into cattle cars. Riding the rails. One way.

Many don't survive the GHASTLY journeys. From factory farms. Same design as Auschwitz. Dachau. Buchenwald. And Birkenau. Meg noticed rows and rows of parallel sheds. And the tracks. To and from those hell holes. On her flights West. Terrifying rides. Frightened ani-mals. Crushed. Frozen. Overheated. Starving. PARCHED and desperate. For water. On the haul to slaughter*houses*. Why slaughter*houses*? Houses are to *live* in. Built to protect. Aren't they? Not for *killing*. Pulled my stump down tight. At these thoughts. The heart-breaking things Meg speaks. Crawled under the back-seat cover. And slept.

Sophie*the*dog always greets us. At Bob's and Nancy's front door. That's the routine. *Whap whap whap.* Her German-Shepherd tail pounds the entryway table. We rumpus. Up goes Nancy's anxiety. Needs her inhaler. But then she pulls herself together. And says "Glad you made it, safely." I sidle up to her. Wag*wag*wag. "Hi, Dori," she replies. But she doesn't give me scratches or pats. Or hugs. To her I'm *justadog*. One she really doesn't care for.

Meg gives me PRIVILEGES. Though. In Vermont. At home I spend nights in a big cage. Humph. On a plaid VELOUR dog pad! In Meg's and

Jack's bedroom. They clamp my crate shut. With vise grips. Because I learned how to shake it open! Um hm. Vise grips. So I don't chew the carpets. When they're asleep. Or play with the trash. Because I'm bored. But at Nancy's and Bob's house I crash. With Meg. Sack out. On the guest bed. Smack dab. In the middle. In the crook of her legs. Don't think Nancy knows. Nope. That I'm on her clean white spread. One place white fur works. In my favor! Or maybe she's figured it out. Just doesn't want to get into it. With Meg. Um hm.

Every day we take long walks. On dirt roads. I sniff bear scents and coyote. Fisher smells. Rabbits. Deer. Newts and foxes. Zig zag zig zag zig zig zag. Poison ivy. Meg yanks me back. Ooph! Mud and burrs. Ticks. Wooly Bear caterpillars. Copper and black. Dewy spiders' webs stick to my nose. Goldenrod. Purple clover and thistles. And cow manure. From the spreader. That drives down the road. To the fields. *Nuph nuph nuph nuph nuph nuph.* "Doricomealong." *Nuph nuph nuph.* Zig zag zig zag. "Dori*heel!*" I want to run. In the fields. And roll. In the dirt. Like we used to do. My brothers and sisters. And I. Yup! Getting it right. At my first home. In Missouri. Ooph!

Just before dinner I made a few passes. At Bob. He has white hair. Kind of wispy. And glasses. That make him look like a bug. He has a stump. Too. With a PROSTHESIS. That's hard-as-rock. Leg ground off. By farm equipment. When he was fourteen. During World War II. He worked in the fields. Supporting his family. While his father the general fought. In Europe. For five years. Now he's tippy. And falls over. Sometimes. So he uses an aluminum walking stick. I put my head. On his lap. Made the little black spots. Above my eyes. Go up and down. Up down. Up down. Gave him my quizzical look. Right spot *up. Down.* Left spot *up. Down.*

At first he laughed. Then he snapped, "Dori, get your head. Off! *My* napkin." Ooph! No "please." Was just trying to be friendly. Maybe I should *grrrowl* at him. To make peace he might pat me. He did once. So there's hope.

"How does Dori hurt your napkin?" Meg asked. Bob doesn't want a *dog.* Touching his ironed India-print napkin. Not even this SINGULAR white dog. Meg PERSISTED: "How is that different from you eating, without washing your hands, after pushing Dori away?" She doesn't like INCONSISTENCY. Bob called Meg OBSTREPEROUS. Said he sure wouldn't want to live. With *her!* "Can't imagine living with *you*, either," she snorted. And went back. To the kitchen. Where she changed her mind. And added *carrots!* To the vegan dinner. Because Bob doesn't like *carrots!* But I dooooo!

Jack thinks all families are SCREWY. But he says that Meg's family is extra extra *extra*screwy. That happens when you have a lot. Of COMPETITIVE people. In one family. Convinced they are EXCEPTIONALLY INTELLIGENT. Ask me. And I'll tell you they're just a bunch. Of know-it-alls. Yup! They are. I could go on!

Meg's family has Tea Party members; progressives; a Mormon; a Christian Scientist; fundamentalists; a whole bunch of atheists and agnostics; artists; lawyers; mechanical engineers; a scrum master; architects; teachers and professors; students; animal-rights, environmental, and social-justice activists; an amputee; members of the NRA; a retired career military officer; veterans; vegans; CARNIVORES; former drug addicts; ex-husbands and ex-wives; Koreans, Scots, Irish, an Austrian and an Australian, and Portuguese; dogs; cats; birds; and a horse; wide people; thin people; short people; tall people; employed and unemployed; hoopsters; video gamers; riders; footballers and a Scottish dancer; only-buy-American-cars people and only-buy-foreign-cars people; PhDs and JDs. No degrees. And *me! Phisst!* Without a pedigree. Um hm. Interesting lot.

When Meg cooks she uses fresh organic vegetables. Doesn't want her family eating pesticides and herbicides. Chemicals. That harm nature. And kill bees. And other beings. Organic fruits and grains. Too. And nuts. She cuts and chops. Grates and slices. Sometimes she snicks her nails. And trims off the tips. Of her fingers. She'll suck on them. For a bit. To ease the pain. And stop the bleeding. Then goes right back at cutting and slicing. Chopping. Peeling. Dicing and mashing. Makes such colorful meals! And tasty! Too.

While she cooks Spike and Grace. And I sit. By her side. Meg gives us chunks. Of raw sweet potato and broccoli. Red and yellow Swiss chard stems. Orange pepper pieces. Purple cabbage leaves. And pale green fennel. Meg says fennel keeps fleas. Off dogs. Um hm. And celery and squash. Carrots. Apples and bananas. But we can't have onions and avocados and grapes. Pistachios. Walnuts. And chocolate. Not even vegan chocolate. *No*siree! All toxic to dogs. Warned Kathryn*the*veterinarian.

My humans have reasons. Why we should be *vegan*dogs. Yup! Protect animals. Protect the planet. And they want to protect *us*! From *cancer*. Persis. Their first Boxer died. Of cancer. In her brain. Bewildered. She stood. With her head in a corner. Between the piano. And the wall. Then Meg read *The China Study*. About the research. That shows how whole-foods plant-based diets can reverse and cure cancer. In humans. Can prevent it! Too. And that gave her the *idea*. Meg always has ideas and theories. And hypotheses. Based on *patterns*. Um hm. Says she learned about patterns. From the attorney. Who helped her and a COLLEAGUE succeed. In a SEXUAL HARRASSMENT lawsuit. Against a university. He said it's easier to win. With patterns. That support the case.

Anyhoo Dr. Campbell wrote *The China Study*. Meg told Jack he's a *big*wig biochemist. In NUTRITIONAL SCIENCE. His book explains cancer is turned *on*. In laboratory animals. And in humans. With animal PROTEIN. Then turned *off*. When they eat only plant protein. And no animal protein. (Animal protein. Meat and dairy! Folks. Got that?) "Poor lab animals," Meg says. "Now there's a cruel irony!"

Boxers and cancer. Seem to go together. Twice Kathryn*the*veterinarian cut TUMORS. Out of Grace. First time she sliced open Gracie's face. Ever so carefully. Along the edge. Of her brown patch. So the incision wouldn't show. And Spike's had cancer. Twice. Ooph! Too much cancer. Like dodging bullets. Meg spent months. Researching plant-based diets. For dogs. Talked with Dr. Campbell. Who trained in veterinary medicine. Before he became a scientist. Then Meg and Jack decided. We would become *vegan*dogs. Hasn't been so bad. Even though we weren't CONSULTED! Mind you.

Dr. Campbell has a professor's chair at Cornell. Maybe like ours. With pink hydrangeas. In front. Of a big window! You think? Spike went to Cornell. Because he BEFUDDLED Kathryn. With his INCESSANT URINATION. She photographed his brain. Not Cushings Disease. "Common cause of INCONTINENCE in Boxers," explained Kathryn. So she sent him. To Cornell. To the Veterinary School of Medicine. Meg's sister Elizabeth went to Cornell. Long before Spike. But she wasn't cured of anything. Nope! Studied Landscape Architecture. And she's vegan. When Spike went. To Cornell. The veterinarians loved him. *To*pieces. Let him run. Free! In their office area. While they figured out why he leaked. Now he's given a SYNTHETIC HORMONE. Twice a day. Eye drops. For DIABETES INCIPITUS. Bingo! Problem solved. All this. Before I arrived.

For years he peed. Everywhere. Soaked dog beds. Big puddles. Meg's and Jack's blankets and sheets. Pee squirting out. While he ran around the house. Desperate. Confused. *Zig zag zig zag zig zag*. On the carpets. Down the stairs. *Zig zag zig zag*. Across the porch as he raced. Out the door. Meg called it "urinary cursive" and "Spike writing." He dribbled and dripped. And sometimes gushed. He hung his head. In shame. Broke Meg's and Jack's hearts. They still talk. About that time. Once in awhile.

Glad I wasn't around to see Spike desperate. And watch Meg go all crazy. Washing. Washing. Washing. Bedding. Floors. Stairs. Porch flagstones. Hauling the heavy carpets. Out for cleaning. Every few weeks. Jack remembers that Spike. A very CONSCIENTIOUS dog. Became depressed. Our humans grew DISTRAUGHT. He'd look up at them with MELANCHOLY eyes. And refused to go. Into the bedroom. Where we stay. While Meg and Jack teach. Fearing he'd wet their bed. Again. Now that he's cured. He's an *eversohappy* dog!

Today I went to see Kathryn*the*veterinarian. She's PETITE and cute. Meg told me not mention her looks. At all! Ooph! Says it's sexist. To describe a woman's APPEARANCE. Especially when it's not PERTINENT.

To the story. Ooph! Ooph! Ooph! Anyhoo she's the boss of the clinic. She. Who cut out *my* uterus. And *Godonlyknows* what she did with it! Why my humans let her. What *were* they thinking? Probably weren't! Just went with the spay-neuter program! Humph! Anyhoo Kathryn runs MARATHONS. Today I wanted to *bite* her. Do damage.

While we waited to see Kathryn. We watched a woman. Smack her little dog. In the face. With a rolled-up newspaper. Each time he tried to climb. Into her lap. Because he was scared. *Thawp!* People just sat there. *Thwap!* No one said a word. Not even the clinic staff. Who looked away. *Thwap!* Ooph! Wanted to *chew off that nasty lady's hands*. Just leave *her*. With *stumps*!

She *thwapped* her dog three times. Then Meg asked the woman, "Would you like to be smacked in the face every time you wanted your companion to comfort you?" The woman stared at Meg. As if she couldn't quite figure out the awful smell my human reminded her of. The hitting stopped. That's my Meg! Next I studied pictures. On the bulletin board. Of heartworms. In dogs' hearts. All stringy like spaghetti. Wondered what it would feel like to have tangles. In my heart? That could *kill* me!

Meg asked Kathryn why my sides have pink circles. "From loss of fur," she explained. "Dori has SEASONAL FLANK ALOPECIA common-to-Boxers." Then out of the blue Kathryn said, "Dori, *you* are *fat*." She could have told us. That MELATONIN can make a dog's fur grow back. But no! Instead she said I'm *fat*! Humph. (Meg figured out the melatonin thing. Later. All by herself! Now my sides have *lotsoffur!*)

Anyhoo Kathryn insisted I lose *ten* pounds. That's .1333 percent. Of my body weight. What *am* I supposed to do? Eat fewer carrots. Each week? Crinkles my whiskers. Rubs my fur the wrong way. Kathryn told Meg to give me a half cup. Of kibble. Twice a day. With my vegetable and fruit smoothies. Half of what I'm served now!

Then she jabbed a HYPODERMIC needle. Into my rump. Ooph! So I don't get rabies. She cooed, "Dori, you're sweet." "Lady," I wanted to say, "Brown nosing doesn't make up. For the insult. Leave that to the dogs!" *Grrrrr! Fat!* Takes a lot for me to hold back. Humans can be so rude. Real TWERPS! Including Meg and Jack. Who only feed me *half* as much food. Now. Even though I'm not *fat*. Not. *Not. NOT!* I have *muscles!* I have *mass*. I have SIGNIFICANCE! Like my mom. In Missouri. Humph. Humph. Humph. And HUMPH! I miss my mom. Who'd lick my ears to say she loves me. Just the way I am!

Rain. A *splendid* day. With mud! In the garden. Little wrinkled leaves. On the maples and oaks stretch open. Rolled-up hosta shoots grow taller. And unfurl. Right before my eyes! *Yessiree!* The yard has a carpet. Of purple violets. And yellow dandelions. That will turn into fluffy white balls. Which drift away. When I sniff. *Nuph nuph nuph.*

And after the storm. Scents in the yard will smell extra smelly. Worms will have crawled. Out of the ground. Onto the walks. And asphalt. So they don't drown. Meg places them back. Ever so gently. On the grass. And dirt. Before they shrivel. Dry out and die.

Tulips will bloom. In random places. Never the same. From year to year. Last March a yellow one opened. Under the orange azalea. Two red and white tulips appeared. In the pachysandra. Pink ones by the trunk. Of the white Rose of Sharon. Meg says squirrels dig up the bulbs. *Squirrels!* Ooph! The thought of them winds me up. And rebury them. Spike eats their petals. Tulips don't stand a chance. In our yard.

With nightfall comes spring snow! *Phisst! Prance prance prance!*

Last week we had a surprise. Meg shouted to Jack, "It's a *miracle*." The dogwood had bloomed. At last. Big white stars. For the life of me I can't figure out. What that tree has to do. With *dogs*.

For Jack's birthday. Meg planted the dogwood. Says it's looked BEDRAGGLED. Until she began pruning it. A tall stick. ASKEW. With SCRAWNY branches. Before I arrived. At last the tree has leafy limbs. And white blossoms. Reaching out. Floating. Over the garden. Sort of JAPANESE-looking. ETHEREAL. As my human would say. Truth is I considered chewing down the dogwood. When it still looked a little rangy. Same as two other saplings I cut my teeth on. Lucky for that tree it flowered.

The woman's got a thing. About pruning trees. And bushes. Into shapes. The mulberry tree's now a huge umbrella. The Scotch pine has poufs. She cleaned up the Roses of Sharon and yews. With loppers and clippers. Japanese-y. Too. Not so scruffy. And she cut the SCRAGGLY hedge. Into round lollypops.

Grace has been flapping her ears. All morning. *Whup whup whupity whup.* I checked them out. One stinks. *Whup whupity whup.* Meg used an eyedropper. Put HYDROGEN PEROXIDE down her ear canal. Ooph! Grace shook her head. *Violently! Whup whup whupity whup.* Flung the peroxide right back out. Jack hugged her tight. While Meg soaked up blood. With cotton balls. I licked her ear. *Lick lick lick.* Seemed to soothe her. *Lick lick lick.* And relieve the pain. Grace fell. Into a deep sleep. After Kathryn treated the yeast infection. That gave her the ache.

Grace is patient. Good natured. And anxious. Especially when Meg's on a rant. About the environment. And how humans treat animals. About eating deadly meat and dairy. Her voice tense. Pitched higher. Then Grace pants. *Uhuh uhuh uhuh. Uhuh uhuh.* Me. Too. Yeah yeah yeah. *I.* As well. Otherwise she's busy TALLYING. Keeping things. On the up and up. Um hm. Meg and Jack call her the "*littleaccountant.*" Because she watches who gets what. How many ice cubes Jack hands out. To each of us. How many almonds. Carrots. And apple slices. For snacks. Grace knows. When she's been shorted. She stares *hard*. At those two. Follows them around. Panting. *Huh uhuh uhuh uhuh uhuh.* When the count's off. We dogs know fair. From not.

Grace never lets her titanium knees stop her. Climbing steps looks painful. She hops up. Back legs all stiff. And SPLAYED. Has difficulty skooching her rear end down to pee. Because her knees don't bend so well. She tries to join our rumpuses. And mad dashes. Around the back yard. But can't keep up. So she barks and barks. Cheers us on.

Even after escaping the WHELPING BOX. And bouncing. Down the stairs. Of the house. Where she was born. On her white puppy head. With the brown patch over one eye. And a HYSTERECTOMY. Two surgeries. For cancer. And having her back knees rebuilt. With titanium. Grace remains upbeat. An OPTIMIST despite her troubles. Always wags*wags*wags her stump of a tail. She sleeps. Ever so contented. And *snores*!

On the days Meg and Jack stay home. And evenings. She lies. At the top of the stairs. Figured out the best spot. In the house. For getting MAXIMUM attention. Meg kisses her. Rubs her ears. And asks, "How's my Gracie?" As she goes up. And down. While doing chores.

When I arrived. Grace became the middle dog. So Meg and Jack take extra care not to overlook her. Her food bowl's filled first. And before sunrise Grace sneaks up. Onto their bed. *Never* kicked off. *No*siree. I used to bang my crate door. Over that. *Bangity bangity bang. Bangity bang.* And bark. *Eeeeeeeunh! Eeeeeeeunh!* And whine. *Nnnnnnnn.* But now I understand.

We each have our privileges. I sleep with Meg on the bed. In Vermont. Spike has *extra*long walks. With Jack. These things I understand. I do. Which makes me think I'm *growing*up. I'm almost as tall as Grace. Um hm. Not so much a puppy. Not anymore. And I bet. When Meg suddenly realizes this. She'll cry. Little snuffle noises. Just like she does whenever Ellie leaves. For Utah. *Snuf snuffle snuf.* And every autumn. As the geese fly south. She cries hard. On our trips to Vermont. When we see the pigs and cows. Goats and chickens. Being hauled to slaughter. *Snuffle snuffle snuffle.* "Oh Dori," she weeps. I lean over. And lick her. Lots. *Lick lick lick.* On the cheek. *Lick lick lick.*

Meg's friend Janet. With curly *red*hair. Planted *her* vegetable garden. Already! Peas. Swiss chard. Spinach. Weeks ago! Meg says Janet's always on-top-of-things. Energetic. Organized. Fit. Vegan. And *highly* productive. Maybe peppy *red*curls do that to a person!

I tried to force the issue. Here. At our house. Hopped the garden fence. And stood. Where my vegetables should be growing. All I got from Jack was "Dori*outofthere*." Humph. Meg says the seedlings have not been delivered. Yet. To our co-op. She doesn't seem to be in any hurry. "Global Warming," she says, "means a longer growing season. No rush." Soon Meg and I head back. To Vermont. I know we'll leave. In a day or two. She's making lists. Back to her parents' house. Where Nancy grows apples and raspberries. Blueberries and edible flowers. Nancy doesn't plant a vegetable garden.

Birds. Birds. *Birds*! *Phisst*! I *love* birds. Early this morning. In the long shadows and *damp*grass. And dandelions. I ran HELTER SKELTER. Round the back yard. Chasing a blue jay. I watched a hawk circle. Overhead. And robins. With plump copper chests. Fly *flufl flufl flufl*. To feed their three hungry chicks. Nesting. In the mulberry tree. Two cardinals swooped down. Onto the lollypop hedge. Then up. To the telephone lines. And higher. Into the *old*oak. Calling their mates *uree uree ureee chipchipchipchip chew chew cheeew*. Wrens hopped. On the mossy patio. And fled. Whenever I came near. Humph.

Meg would like to have a bird friend. A crow. Who'd hang out. In our back yard. But the town has *laws*. Only allowed to *kill* crows. Can't be friends. With them. *Grrrrr*! Snarls my whiskers. Just want to *bite* the members. Of the town council. Bite. Bite. *Biiite*! Rip their pants. Who make cruel and useless rules. Humph.

Crows remember faces. For years. Especially people. They don't like. Those who've hurt them. Hurt their tribe. Called a "Murder of Crows." Once humans believed they were OMENS. Of death. Meg told Jack. But crows are true and devoted. Only attack meanies. Before I arrived she tried. To help a crow. With a broken wing. And a bald head. He dropped. From the oak. *Wayuphigh*. Meg named him Rufus.

A bird vet couldn't heal him. Saved a pigeon she named Bob. Though. And a raccoon. Yup! Another one. She likes to tell that story.

One cold spring day. Spike ran back and forth. In the yard. With a muddy knob. Of fur. In his mouth. He brought the creature. To Jack. Jack handed the little one. To Meg. She wiped the animal clean. And saw that Spike had been carrying. A *baby*raccoon! She put the almost-frozen cub. Under her shirt. He thawed. And cried little chirping noises. Meg wiped his stomach. With a warm damp cloth. So he'd learn to pee. Since he didn't have his mother. To lick him. And teach him how to urinate. He slept on flannel. Snug in a box. Meg named him. Or her. Pete.

Then Meg found a woman. Who REHABILITATES raccoons. The woman took Pete with her. Every day. To work. Until the kit grew up. And returned to the fields and woods. That was *long* ago. Meg says Pete's probably dead now. Wild raccoons only live two to three years. In captivity they can live twenty years. Longer than dogs!

Whenever we go to Vermont. Meg greets each SOLITARY hawk. Perched. On a highway light. "Hello hawk," she says. And "Hello!" To the wild turkeys. Too. And the Canada geese. And their goslings, "Hello geese." Last time we drove. To Vermont. We saw a dead eagle. Lying broken. In the breakdown lane. Feathers waved. As we sped by.

Meg told Jack another *long*-ago story. About a mockingbird. Named Sidewalk. For the place. Where she found him. A little ball of fuzz. Fell. From his nest. Late one spring. In Baltimore. She raised the bird. Taught him to fly. Sitting on her finger. Moved her hand. Every day. For a couple of weeks. Up and down. Until he fledged. And sneaked him. In a picnic basket. Onto the bus. And into her office at City Hall. Where she worked. For the mayor. The security guards smiled. And looked the *other*way. After Meg explained. That Sidewalk ate. Every twenty minutes.

Riding the bus. To work. And home. Meg sat in the back. So the drivers couldn't hear him screech. With excitement. No birds allowed.

On public transit. Sidewalk entertained the riders. Who asked to peek. Inside the basket. At City Hall he ran back and forth. On her desk. Soiled papers. Flew about. Looking for handouts. Perched on the shoulders. Of staff. And screamed. For food. "Hizonor" heard the COMMOTION. During a budget meeting! And roared, "Get that God*damn*bird. Out. Of. Here!"

Soon after Meg released Sidewalk. Into the back yard. For two days he yelled. From a tree. For her? Who knows. Probably so. And as he ran. Up and down the backyard path. Beside the flower gardens. And raspberry bushes. Then one evening she heard his voice grow faint. And called after him. He returned. For the night. But the next day. He flew away. For a few weeks she saw a mockingbird. Near the back porch. Watching. Waiting. For Meg? Then he disappeared. The mayor died. Sidewalk must be dead. Too. Such a *long*ago story.

Now Maggie*the*cockatiel lives in a big cage. In the corner. Of our bright-blue dining room. Meg chose the color. Because she liked the name. Of the shade of paint. "Myth." Anyhoo Maggie lives in a cage. Between two Korean rice chests. Where she sings. Observes the world. And warns us. Security systems don't work as well. As Maggie. Nope. They don't. UPS trucks arrive. Maggie *squawks*. Cars pull. Into the driveway. She screeches. Dogs trot by. With their humans. That bird goes on high alert. She's no good after dark. Though. Grows quiet. When the sun sets. Once in a while Maggie flies. About the house. Chews venetian blinds. Frames on paintings. And papers. On the kitchen table.

We corner her. Spike and Grace and I. (Just dropped that *I*. Into the sentence. Smooth like. Um hm.) Whenever she settles. On the floor. After one of her flights. Three black noses. Sniff her gray and yellow face. With orange cheeks. She screams. Until Jack pushes into the crowd. And lifts Maggie. To his shoulder. Where she rides around high*high*high. Because Jack stands six foot five. Then she swoops down. Onto her perch. And Jack closes the cage door.

That Maggie can't be LIBERATED. Saddens my humans. They say they'll never have another jailed bird. Never*ever*never! Again. Even though they love her chirps. And whistle. In return. Once she escaped and fled. Into the back yard. Free. And clung to the trunk. Of the *old*oak. For awhile. Probably stunned by her slip. From life behind bars. But not so high Meg couldn't grab her. Before she became a hawk's meal.

Feels like we're getting there. Jack raked soggy leaves. From the garden beds. Yesterday Meg began to weed the plot. Yippee yippee yippee! Dug out buckets and buckets. Of crab grass. Purslane and dandelions. Meg doesn't pull out all the dandelions. Because the greens go into salads. And she adds the roots. To smoothies. For Grace. To boost her IMMUNE SYSTEM. Some people make purslane tea. My humans don't bother.

Finally those two discussed the vegetables they'll grow. This year. So far I've heard cabbage. Collards. Tomatoes and arugula. Eggplants. Peppers. And Brussels sprouts! Makes me want to *bounce bounce bounce*! And jump high as the top. Of the mulberry tree. And nip Meg's fingers. Which I do. When I'm worked up. And *prance prance prance*! Vegetables! Oh vegetables! *Phisst!*

Week after next we'll visit one of the world's most famous nutritional scientists. Dr. T. Colin Campbell. Remember him? Who says it's best to eat plants. Only! No meat. No dairy. No eggs. No fish. He has a chair. At Cornell. But you know that. Already!

Meg will drive her high-school student Kenneth. To meet Dr. Campbell. At his house. For his senior project Kenneth's becoming a vegan *body*builder. With a sweet smile. Dr. Campbell invited me! Too. A car ride! Wag*wag*wag. *Phisst!*

Now Kenneth eats fruits. He told Meg. And she told me. And vegetables. Before that he ate chips and fries. Barbecued ribs. Hamburgers and greasy chicken. Hotdogs. Macaroni and cheese. Milkshakes. Pizza. And drank gallons of soda.

In Meg's *Sustainable Living* class he learned about farmed animals' suffering. And brutal slaughter. And how raising animals for food *heats*up the atmosphere. And the oceans. With greenhouse gasses. Yup! UNSUSTAINABLE! From burning fossil fuels to breed and grow cows. Pigs. Chickens. And goats. And crops. For their food. From cutting down rainforests. For grazing cattle. And from the animals. Themselves. The gas from their DIGESTIVE SYSTEMS and waste. All that creates nearly sixty percent. Of all climate-warming EMISSIONS. In the world! Very important organizations say this. Says Meg. Worldwatch Institute and the World Bank. Greenhouse gases like CARBON DIOXIDE. That's CO_2. For short. And methane. That holds up to one hundred times more heat than CO_2. And nitrous oxide. A greenhouse gas. With two hundred and ninety-six times more warming POTENTIAL. Than CO_2. Yikes! And he learned how raising animals. For food. Poisons the environment. With manure and urine filled. With growth hormones. Antibiotics. Pesticides and herbicides. That pass through the animals. Ammonia too. From LAGOONS filled with animals' pee and feces. And something toxic called REACTIVE ORGANICS. That pollute rivers and lakes and oceans. Create dead zones. And the land. And how the farmed-animal industry sprays this poison. Into the air. Because no one knows how to get rid of it. Humans and animals breathe this deadly stuff! Ooph! And die.

And when Kenneth realized. That no reason exists to eat animals. No reason to destroy them and the environment. And that the protein and fat. And growth hormones and antibiotics. In meat and dairy can make people sick. That breeding animals to kill them. So humans can eat their flesh and fluids is racist. Because humans think they are superior. And can use us creatures any way they want. He decided to go vegan. He read *The China Study*. And learned how a whole-foods plant-based diet can prevent. And cure deadly and DEBILITATING diseases. Like cancer and diabetes. And heart disease. On the ride to Dr. Campbell's house Kenneth said, "Who wouldn't want to be vegan?"

Together Meg and Kenneth took a course. For doctors. On the health benefits. Of eating plants. Only. She'd come home.

And tell Jack everything they learned. That vegan athletes recover more quickly. In half the time. From exertion. Vegan males have higher TESTOSTERONE levels. Humans lose extra weight. Without trying. Have loads more energy. Than meat and dairy eaters. Vegans don't age. As quickly. Have lower cancer rates. And less dementia. Actually become smarter! Can reverse diabetes. And unclog their arteries. Lower cholesterol. Without drugs. Eating only fruits and vegetables. Grains and nuts.

It surprised them to hear. That dairy is toxic. Increases some cancers. And one-percent milk is less healthy than bacon. *Bacon!* A Group One carcinogen. Right up there with ASBESTOS and PLUTONIUM! And all processed meats. According to the World Health Organization. A strip of bacon has less saturated fat. Than an eight-ounce glass. Of low-fat milk. Meg and Kenneth learned that milk LEACHES calcium. From bones. Weakens them. Not what the dairy industry wants you to believe! That's why. In their advertisements. They put little milk mustaches. On famous faces. All smiley. Looking like they really tucked. Into some kind of healthy and tasty drink. With calcium. That the dairy industry *adds*. But added calcium doesn't do the trick. Folks. *No*siree! Truth is milk drains calcium. From your bones. Countries where humans eat a lot. Of dairy. Have the highest bone-fracture rates. And the most osteoporosis. Yup! And dairy can increase prostate cancer. And ovarian cancer. Meg read about that. After they finished the course. That's what a Harvard study said. Dairy kills.

Many plant foods have lots of calcium. They learned. And more and better protein per pound. Than meat! Um hm. That all plant cells contain protein. Even plant cell walls. Meat's made from plant protein! Folks. Think about it! And that the world's strongest weight lifter is vegan! And the world's strongest animals. Eat only plants. That plant protein is *complete*! And SOLUBLE. Not animal protein. *No no no*! And animal foods gunk up human arteries. Make GEL PLAQUES. That *pop*! Ooph! And become blood clots. Bingo! That cause strokes! Animal fats and cholesterol clog arteries. Causing heart attacks. And dementia. And loads of other problems.

Kenneth struggles to stick. To a whole-foods plant-based diet. Sometimes he says, "It's too much work." Meg imagines it must be hard. Being a plant-eating teenager. Not cool being different. And the *only* one. In your family. Who eats plants. And no animals. Probably the *only* one eating vegan food. In the whole 'hood. Where finding fresh vegetables can be difficult. That's why they're called "food deserts." Dr. Campbell will talk. To Kenneth. About his senior project. While I sniff around his yard.

Back to Vermont. The day after Meg takes her students. To Farm Sanctuary. Near the Finger Lakes. Where rescued farmed animals live out their natural lives. Safe from humans. Anyhoo Meg and Jack bought an old house. A mess! In New Hampshire. Where you "live free or die." Like New Hampshire's wild animals. Who live free. Until they're hunted! And trapped! Then die! For humans' EGO GRATIFICATION. That's what the animal-rights people say. The hunters and trappers insist it's "conservation." "Tradition." "Sport." "Food for their families." Well animals have families to feed. Too. I'd like to remind those hunters. Trappers. And humans who fish. And it's no sport. When one side has all the weapons. Animals want to care for. And protect *their* kin. *Grrrrr*! A satisfied look. More than a hint. Crosses Meg's face. When she reads. About a hunted animal. Killing a hunter. Um hm.

Our *new*old house is not too far. From Bob's and Nancy's and Sophie*the*dog's and Willi*the*cat's home. In Vermont. On the other side. Of the Connecticut River. Meg and I stay with them. While we check on the RENOVATION. No one has lived in the one-hundred-year-old house. For years. Furnace? On the fritz. Wiring no good. Needs insulation. New windows. A garage. And a big porch. Like the one we have now. Doors. Roof. Paint. Ooph! Ooph! Ooph! I know. Because I go. With Meg. Who talks to the CONTRACTORS. Anyhoo I like the house. I do. *Phisst*!

It has tall windows. That nearly touch the floors. Grace and Spike and I'll be able to see what's up. With the neighbors! We'll have room. For indoor rumpuses. And a grand yard. For chases. The attached barn has an outhouse. A two-holer. Meg says that will go! And a skunk. Musicians live next door. With a yappy little dog. Yup! Another one. They give concerts. Every summer! And have a tall wood fence. Kind of MID-CENTURY MODERN. Meg stands on her tippy toes to chat. With them. I peek. Between the slats.

But I'll be farther away. From Missouri. Meg said to Jack. And my furry family. Ooph! Must lie down. Makes me feel faint. My ears droop. Stump drop. Wag. Wag. Maybe my brothers and sisters don't live there. Anymore. Gone. Like Pepper and *I*.

Today Meg and her *Sustainable Living* class ride a yellow school bus. To Farm Sanctuary. I want to go. With them. But I *must* stay home. In my crate. It's not fair. Animals don't have cages. At the sanctuary. Why me? I know! I know! GRAMMATICAL error! "Phooey on you," I want to say. Take your "*I*" and shove it! *Eeeeeeunh*. Phooey. Phooey. *Phooey*! Leap*leap*leap. At Meg. "Dori*sit*!" Humph. Leap*leap*leap. "Dori*off*!" Bump into Meg. Bump bump *bump*! "Damn*you*Dori!" Try a new TACTIC. Go and search for my ratty cloth fox. And bring it. To Meg. But she's too busy. Packing her vegan lunch. And checking students' permission slips to play. With me. I don't budge.

"Dori*move*!" says Meg. On her third try at opening the kitchen door. I don't care. That she asked me. All *sweet*like. The first time. Humph! "Dori*move*. You can't go. To Farm Sanctuary. With the students. And that's *that*." Ooph! I want I want *I want* to visit the cows. Who were rescued. From slaughter houses. And dead piles. From farmers. Who abused them. I want to play. With the piglets Sebastian and Jane. The sheep. Goats. And ducks. With the rabbits. Rescued. From dreadful lives. In laboratories. Where their necks would have been broken. After they served no purpose. And the chickens. With burned-off beaks. Saved from being crammed. Into small wire cages. And from huge sheds. Oooh. The STENCH! Stuffed with so many birds they cannot move. Then marketed as "cage-free." I want to watch the tom turkeys fan their tail feathers.

Meg says the sanctuary animals were *traumatized*. In their former lives. Then I hear the LITANY. Again! How they were imprisoned. Like all the others. On factory farms and dairies. Bashed. Slammed against concrete floors. Castrated. Stabbed. Assaulted. Molested. Amputated. Filthy. Sick. Cattle fed sawdust. Fish guts. Chicken GUANO. And OFFAL from slaughtered animals. Pigs. Too. Who naturally eat vegetables. Mostly. Forced to eat animal waste. And old newspapers soaked. With RANCID animal fat. Shoved with fork lifts. When they fall down. Too sick and weak to move. Dragged away. And left to die. Beaten and kicked down the chutes. To the killing floors. Where bolts shot. Into their brains only stun them. So they can be sliced open alive. For *tastier*meat! And bigger profits!

It's all too much. For a puppy to hear. "But we *must* take responsibility. For this horror," Meg insists. "Dori, it's so easy to be *complicit* in evil. If we pretend it doesn't exist. Shrug and justify it as tradition. And culture. As if they were cast in stone. Like eating animals! Humph. Insist that the only way we get enough protein is to consume others' bodies. Believe that God gave humans DOMINION over creatures to do whatever they want to them. We're wrong, if we don't stop this. Especially when there is no need. It's the 'no need' part that makes it wrong."

With my head. On her pillow. On Meg's and Jack's bed. My lids shut. I half listen. Wait for the blast. To be over. Drop off. Wake just when she ends. "And now those who've been rescued need peace," Meg explains. "Dogs make them anxious." But I would be so happy. At Farm Sanctuary. Spin! And *prance*! Bounce. And bark *Eeeeeeunh!* Lick my new friends. And bow down. With my rump in the air. And wag*wag* and wiggle. Twist myself. Into knots. Asking them to play. *Eeeeeeeunh.*

Yesterday Kenneth and I rode. To the shore. Of Lake Cayuga. Meg drove. To visit Dr. Campbell. I sat in back. With Kenneth. He scratched me. Behind my ears. Gave me vegan treats. I licked him. *Lick lick lick.* He saved a hurt seagull. From the school parking lot. *My* friend! My own special *new*friend! I think he likes me. Too. I dooo!

High above the lake Dr. Campbell's house sits. On a hill. With a vegetable garden! Neat rows. No weeds. Um hm. Meg and Jack still haven't planted theirs. Weeds have returned. Where vegetables should be growing. Weeds. As high as my knees.

A white fence protects Dr. Campbell's garden. So the rabbits and woodchucks can't chew the plants. He and Kenneth sat. On the deck. Talked and ate fruit. And laughed. Meg and I rested. Under a tree. With long thorns. And watched two goldfinches. And a magpie. Meg said magpies live in Korea. She went there. To research international adoption. Human trafficking. Actually. The Korean War. And U. S. IMPERIALISM. And how they connect. Met a Korean artist. Married him. Second husband. Now Nora the movie director is making a movie. *The Hanji Box*. About their awhile*ago* story.

Meg's married three men. Ooph! *Three.* Jack says, "I'm her current spouse!" She's a *handful*. I can see that. I wouldn't want to be married. To her. Jack's patient. Calms Meg. Rubs her shoulders. She laughs. Even when he pokes fun. At her FOIBLES. In his gentle way. With twinkles. In his eyes.

Mrs. Campbell joined us. I snapped at *shiny*black carpenter bees. Who crawled in. And out. Of their holes. In the side of their red house. Then I lay down. And watched busy birds fly. From tree to tree. Chirping. Breezes stirred the leaves. And grass.

I dozed a bit. Until Dr. Campbell walked over to speak. With Meg. Startled me. I growled. Kind of upset my flow. He told her how much Kenneth impresses him. Gave Kenneth his cookbook. Based on his documentary *Forks over Knives*. And told Kenneth that he has the most unique. And inspiring story. About becoming a vegan. Against all odds! That he'd *ever* heard. He'll include Kenneth. In his almost-finished new book. I wish Dr. Campbell had a chapter. On *vegan*dogs. Then Kenneth and I could be together! In print!

I slept most of the way home. Except when Meg yelled, "Oh*my*god!" After the car in front of us hit a squirrel. Who WRITHED all over the road. In EXCRUCIATING pain. As she died. "Oh*my*godoh*my*godoh*my*god!"

Before the thunderstorm we went. For a late afternoon walk. Earlier than usual. Meg was quite CHIPPER. Until I almost *yanked* her arm. Out of its SOCKET. Went for a yappy little dog. Ooph! Yappy little dogs rearrange my fur. "Damn*you*Dori!" Ooph! Ooph! Ooph!

Anyhoo she recovered. We trotted along. For a while. Then slowed a bit. Meg listened. Seems a change has come. Over our neighborhood. "It's quieter," she said. "Not so many leaf blowers." I hadn't noticed. A dog doesn't hear so well. With squirrels. In her sight. "Dori*heel*." *Nuph nuph nuph.* "Dori*walk*." *Nuph nuph nuph.* Zig zag zig zag. *Nuph nuph.* "Listen, *Dog*." Now that's serious. Calling me "*Dog*!" Humph.

We pulled it together. Again. For a bit. Then *chic. Chic. Chic. Chic. Chic. Chicchicchic.* A practically horizontal woman. Pushing a grass-cutting CONTRAPTION. Caught my attention. Never seen one of *those* before. Usually a guy. With a gut. Sits on a green machine. So big it barely fits. Into the yard. Burning fossil fuels. And grinds down the lawn.

Next we saw a man. Yanking weeds. From his yard. Not MANEUVERING the usual two-wheel thingamajig around. Spewing weed killer. And INSECTICIDES. People spread that stuff *everywhere*. Around here. Even *on* the *sidewalks*. So I have to walk on it! Poisons humans. Poisons dogs. Birds. Bees and deer. Mice. Rabbits! Kids. You name it. Meg and I see lots. And lots. Of dead birds. On their backs. Feet in the air. Or lying on their sides. Stiff. With their little toes curled tight. Meg says lawn chemicals did them in.

She studied the neighbors' vegetable gardens. That have sprung up. In front yards. Now if Meg were like me. Ooph. *I*. She'd bounce. And *prance prance prance*! And tie herself. Into knots. Over all these humans. Growing plants to eat! But she probably thought, "Not enough! Not fast enough! And they probably eat meat and dairy!" Such a *pill*. She says the word's CURMUDGEON. Humph.

Things are looking up. Though. Everywhere. Changes. Even in the United States government. And among Meg's students. Who went to Farm Sanctuary. A few told her they've stopped eating animals. And their dead embryos and fluids. And one of the teachers. Too. Says she's REEVALUATING her life. After meeting the cows and pigs. And goats. Chickens. Geese and turkeys. Saved from family and factory farms. And slaughterhouses. And the rabbits saved. From experiments. And cosmetics testing.

At the Post Office. Meg bought new stamps. With the words "Heart Health." And a drawing of an apple. And a kale leaf. On them. Meg showed me. Really excited. Waved them. Under my nose. A red and a green blur. And there's more! The United States' government's DIETARY GUIDELINES removed the word "meat." In its place. On the new MyPlate chart is the word "protein." Um hm. Next says Meg, "The circle labeled 'milk' will go." She's certain. Dairy's on its last legs. According to my know-it-all human. Except in China. Where the dairy industry is pushing "their" products. Just like the tobacco industry. Before them. Elsewhere plant-based milks now outsell organic cows' milk! And dairies are closing down. Right and left.

Saturday young vegetable plants. From the public market. Will be tucked into the garden. At*last*! I'll run around the backyard. With Spike and Grace. While Meg and Jack set them in rows! And *ooooooh*! Summer begins three weeks from today. And my humans will stay home. Until September! Makes me go all waggy. So much to consider! In the *flower*chair.

Something big. Yes. *Big*! As in EARTH-SHATTERING. Has been happening. In Meg's family. Like knock-you-out-of-your-*flower*chair *big*. Nancy cooks vegan dinners. Once in a while. And Thanksgiving and Christmas. At their house have gone vegan. Now that's *big*. But I'm talking HUGELY*big*.

Meg's sister Elizabeth. The vegan. Telephoned just before flying away. To the other side. Of the world. She said, "James called. I think you have a victory." Elizabeth's the middle child. Everyone CONFIDES in her. Meg's the oldest. James. *Number*two and born on *Meg's* birthday. Ooph! She crawled after him. When he was a baby. Bit him. On his bottom. Right through his diapers. Something a puppy would do! Bite bite *biiiite*! Big red marks. Nancy asked her mother, "Why does James have WELTS?" Sneaky Meg. Um hm. Like Spike. Nipping me. Does it on the sly. Chomp.

Meg was worse than Spike. Though. When James was a little boy. She stuck a sharp pencil. Into his cheek. Jealousy! And stapled his thumb. To a piece of paper. Meg had to share birthday cakes. With her brother. And *her* first bicycle. Too. Then he went away. To boarding school. Bob and Nancy warned her, "Watch out! Someday he'll be much bigger than you!"

Now James has a beard. Always-in-charge. Ever so tall. And strong. But Meg worries he just might KEEL over. *Any*day. Today! Or tomorrow. From clogged arteries. He was engaged to a woman. Who baked cakes. *Lots* of cakes. And cookies. "A twit," said Meg. For having fed her brother. So much animal fat. Like butter and milk. And eggs. I would never say *any*thing so SNARKY. And mean.

She told that to Jack. Otherwise Meg kept her mouth shut. About the cakes and cookies. And the woman. James doesn't like his sister telling him. How to be healthy. Or anything else. Oh no. In his deep voice he says, "I think this conversation is over." In his emails he writes, "This thread has come to an end." Ooph! Ooph! Ooph! But she only wants her brother to live. A long *long*time. And healthy. That's why she hammered him. About eating a whole-foods plant-based diet. Then she gave up.

He's the brother who shot hoops. And played ice hockey. With her. At night. Under the lights. On Occum Pond. And they biked the Kancamagus Highway. Together. Over the White Mountains. All the way. To Mount Desert Island. Off the coast of Maine. In shirts. Stained. With blood. From black fly bites. Their relationship's a little PRICKLY. Bob calls Meg a PRICKLY PEAR. Even so. She doesn't want to lose James. Um hm. I think she's meanest. And most PERSISTENT. When she's scared. I wish I could see my brothers. Again. And sisters. Too. Chase them! Bite them! Like Meg bit James.

A few nights ago he telephoned. Asked how much vitamin B12 to take. The woman must have known something was up. James almost never seeks advice. She told him, "2500 MICROGRAMS. Once a week." All of us humans and dogs need vitamin B12. It comes from micro-organisms. That live. In the soil. Meat eaters get B12 from dirty plants the animals eat. Um hm. Vegetarians and vegans wash their vegetables and fruit. Before eating them. Wash off the microorganisms. Don't get enough B12. And trouble can happen. Like PERNICIOUS ANEMIA. Ooph! Memory loss. And the runs. You could become agitated. And so weak you can't walk. Makes my fur hurt. My knees wobble. At the thought of no *walks*. Meg tells everyone, "Take B12!"

James told Meg he has GOUT. Meg says gout sounds like something old English dukes have. In BBC productions. How would she know? We don't watch television. Meg and Jack don't even own a TV. James's doctor told him, "Drink more milk." To cure gout? That struck Meg dumb. Imagine her *speechless*! Then she spit, "More milk? *Damn!*" This was going to be good. My human was MIFFED. "Maybe the dairy industry paid for that guy's medical training," she fumed. "Maybe he wants James to increase his chances of getting prostate cancer. By *fifty percent*! So he can make money off that, too!" She helped James find vegan cures. For gout. Raw apple cider vinegar. And *NO* milk. Gout gone!

Next thing you know Bob emailed Meg, "Your brother's instructing *me!* On *The China Study*." Soon after that James knocked her. For a loop. He emailed, "I've read one hundred pages of Campbell's book.

I'm convinced. I'm going vegan. Don't toot your horn." So Meg replied, "Toot toot! Toot toot! Toooooot!"

A good week. Mostly. I ate the buds on the pink peony bush. By the back porch door. And got away with it! Because pale pink flowers don't interest Meg. Shook the vice grips. Off my crate. Last night. Um Hm. And slept on my humans' bed. Thought up a new angle. For retrieving the Nylabone. Too. That Spike nicks. From me. Goes like this. Lick lick lick my human a whole lot. Make Spike jealous. *Lick lick lick.* Spike drops the bone. And tries to out*lick* me. Slobbers all over Jack's or Meg's face. I grab it. Yup!

One thing I didn't manage to do this week. Didn't chew off the fat buds. On the tall stems. Of the yuccas. I've been wanting to. Ever so much. But you-know-who caught me. Eyeing them. Read my mind. "Damn*you*D*o*r*iget*the*hell*away*from*m*yy*uccas." Ooph! Ooph! Ooph! That woman has a temper! And no apology. This time.

Last Saturday we had baths. Grace and Spike. And I. Oooooh! Got it right! Without thinking twice. *I. I. I.* The pronoun for *me*. Dori*dog*. Subject of the sentence. And this book! *Yes*siree! Bath time with Meg. In the pink tub. In the 1940s pink and green tiled bathroom. Where our hydrangea chair would look *so*pretty. Kind of goes with the pink and green MOTIF. You like that? Motif!

I sound like those home-decorating and real-estate staging ladies. Who write advice columns. For magazines. About where to put POTPOURRI. And how to group pictures. On walls. And place pillows. On sofas. How to arrange scented candles. That VOLATIZE PHTHALATES. That cause cancer. And come in stinky-smelling stuff. Like soaps and perfumes. Shampoos. And lotions. Detergents. Antiperspirants. Dryer sheets. Ooph! Ooph! Ooph! We dogs hate perfume-y smells. Give us fresh pee to sniff. And feces. Any day!

Anyhoo as I was saying. When we three wriggle. On our backs and laze. In the dirt. Then track it. Into the house. That RANKLES my human. She huffs, "Jack, the dogs *must* have *baths*. Now!" First I'm washed. Next Grace. Spike's last. We go all stiff. When Jack lifts us. Into the tub filled. With warm soapy water. Meg soaks us. And squirts on lots of shampoo. Organic shampoo. Plant-based. Unscented. Cruelty-free. Of course! No phthalates! And scrubs and scrubs. And *scruuuuuubs*. Until the soap bubbles turn grey. I lean into Meg. My head. On her shoulder. Feel all tingly. Then she hoses me down.

Jack rubs us dry. With old towels. We shake off. *Whup whup whupity whup*. Race around the house. Ooooooh! Soooo good to be clean. Feel *zippy*! Jump onto Meg's and Jack's bed. Jump off the bed. Jump onto the bed. Jump off. On. Off. On. Grace pushes our dog cushions. Into a pile. Jump onto the pile. Race around the dining table. Chasing Spike. Scramble up the stairs. And HURTLE down. *Tump tump tump tumpitytump*.

More mice crises. At school. Necks broken. Yup! That's what the principal told the faculty. At their weekly meeting. Snap traps. And she *laughed*, "Ha ha." Said, "Sorry all you animal rights people." In her little girl voice. That she uses. When she's done something to annoy us. Who make her feel guilty. Sorry? Meg thought the principal seemed quite pleased. With her announcement. "Ha ha." And she wore a small odd smile. For just a moment. Actually a *smirk*. Like the one. On the face. Of the student. Who helped the history teacher. Kill the mouse. With a recycling bin.

Meg thinks the principal doesn't like having plant-based eaters. On her faculty. And students going vegan. Doesn't like Meg's *Sustainable Living* class. Either. Oh no. Maybe all that makes her feel like she's not a good person. Because she eats meat. And dairy. And wears tall black leather boots! And that's a very bad feeling. The "I'm not*agoodperson*" feeling. Sometimes I have the "not*agooddog*" feeling. When Meg says, "*Dooorrri*" in her low growly voice. After I've chewed her shoes.

My humans teach at the same school. They DETEST those two-hour Tuesday meetings. The principal expects everyone to play get-to-know-you games. And read INSPIRATIONAL QUOTATIONS. Don't participate. And she takes note. Onto her shit list you go. "Not collegial" will be on Meg's year-end evaluation. Meg said to Jack, "This is a *control issue* gussied up as team-building." I say it's the same as when my humans gave me treats. *Only* after I followed orders! Um hm. Seems those two have relaxed. Though. Now they give us treats. When *we* ask!

At some meetings. The principal mentions how much she enjoys eating ribs and fried chicken. And steak. "Ha ha." She goes to church. A lot. And plays the organ. I wonder about that. About the connection. Between people who enjoy eating and wearing murdered animals. And go to church. Meg says it reminds her of white slave owners. Who were oooh-*sooooo*-pious. Frederick Douglass. An escaped slave. Abolitionist. And vegan. Talked about those oooh-*sooooo*-pious white Christian owners. Of human chattel. In his autobiography. I'd lie on Meg's stomach. While she read Frederick's book. There's a picture of him on the cover. Wild hair. Stern face. Meg and Jack talked about those oooh-*sooooo*-pious whites. Who impregnated their black "meat."

Meg says "meat" is a DEROGATORY term for women. So are farmed-animal names. Cow. Chick. Hen. Pig. Goat. When they should be compliments! And that meat eating and abuse of animals and pornography INTERCONNECT. With racism and sexism. And violence toward women. And girls. Who are OBJECTIFIED. By men and advertisers. She'll tell you that enslaving women. And girls. In breeding camps. And the "domestication" of animals. Enslaving and breeding them. Too. Began. At the same time. In the same area. In the Middle East. About 10,000 years ago.

She's a feminist. She should know. About women and animals as commodified objects. About how and why. And what men *do*. To them. As things. (Even some men leaders. In the animal-rights movement. "A dirty, ironic secret," says Meg.) That men try to control animals' bodies. In farming and research. Fishing. And hunting. Which Meg calls "sexual psychopathology." And women's bodies. In the never-ending fight. Over abortion and choice. And with sexual assault. Hes not shes wrote the book. Meg points out. That blames a woman and an animal. For being kicked. Out of Eden. Creating a reason. For men to DISDAIN. Prey on. And dominate them. Meg will tell you all this. Whether you want to hear it. Or not. I know I don't want to. Don't want to understand either! I'm a *dog*! After all.

But maybe I should. I'm an animal *and* female. And *my* uterus was taken out. By a woman. Mind you! "Another cruel irony," Meg admits. Meg who paid for my MUTILATION. Double irony. Ooph! And a double bind. AMPUTATION or OVERPOPULATION and euthanasia. That's the awful PREDICAMENT humans force us dogs and cats. Into.

Anyhoo humans. Especially the male ones. Have this strange NOTION that animals. Including dogs. Are theirs to control. That they have the right to call the shots. Ooph! That violent language. Again. Have that right. With female humans! Too. And when women don't cotton. To the male agenda. They're called "bitches." Female dogs. As well. Called "bitches" by breeders. Yup! Who force them to reproduce. Like the slave women. In breeding camps 10,000 years ago.

Like black slaves in America. A black woman enslaved by Meg's family. Had a blond baby girl. Her mother was probably bred. Meg says, "Let's just call it what it was. *Rape!*" By her owner. Meg's ancestor. Then he took the girl. Trained her to be a house slave. Forced to marry another one of his pieces of property. Yup! Humans thought of as things. Meg's grandfather mentioned that child. In his memoir. Think of our babies. Taken from us. Put on the market.

Meg says she descends from a *nasty*lot. Clan Campbell. Scotland's most brutal clan. *Nasty*lot. Puritans. Who were religious fanatics. Thieves. And murderers. Slaughtered indigenous peoples. WHOLESALE. Left and right. Liked to hang their own. The ones who didn't go along. With the program. And slave traders. Really *nasty*lot. Portuguese. Big into slave trading. Another *nasty*lot. And from slave owners. Ooph! Ooph! Ooph! She admits, "Compassion is not a family trait." And adds, "White privilege made us insensitive. Even cruel." Meg asks, "Do the traits and values of our forefathers and mothers filter down to the present? It seems they do."

Anyhoo the blond slave child REVELATION troubles Meg. Why no one in the family wonders about her? "What came of my black relatives?" she asked Jack. Frederick Douglass had things to say. About people like Meg's forebears. And her *today*family. Too. Um hm! Really important and fiery things. That whites *need to hear*. Still! White humans. Not white dogs! About the INHUMANITY of white privilege. "That causes others GENERATIONAL trauma," says Meg.

Frederick had a black mother. And a white father. Um hm. Sound familiar? His last name is Scottish. The Scots in America. Major slave owners. Douglass means "black stream." Meg says, "Frederick Douglass was an abolitionist. A black stream irrigating the pre- and post-Civil War white conscience." Have no idea what she's talking about. When she says these things. Humph! And anyway this is supposed to be *my*book. Not hers. Not with all her issues. And clever comments. Well at least not the ones I don't understand.

Meg goes stormy. Over all this. And how slave owners used their *own* children. By their female slaves. As DRUDGES and property. Sold them. Too. Thought that was okay. After all the *Constitution* said black people weren't humans. Just three-fifths persons. That's how slavery was written. Into America's FOUNDING DOCUMENT. Not in so many words. Just kind of sneaky*sneaky*. Women and animals? Just so you know. Not in the Constitution. At all. Rights and power given only. To white human male property owners. Humph. And look at the trouble that's caused. War. Racism. Sexism. Poverty. SPECIESISM. CARNISM. Holocausts. Farmed animals. And all those used for human purposes. Classism. Extinction! A least.

Anyhoo most ministers. At the time were cool. With that. Says Meg. With slavery. Even in the Northern churches. Because a lot of its FILTHY LUCRE filled church COFFERS. The whole economy built. With slaves. Whose owners gave money. To the parishes. "Slave owners' SALVE for uneasy consciences," says Meg. "True Christians protect the vulnerable and the weak and those whose voices have been silenced and choices have been denied." They have a commandment "Thou shalt not kill." And a Golden Rule. Too. "But here lies the rub," says my human. "Making lots of money so often results in abusing animals and humans. And the planet. The pursuit of wealth requires a kind of ANIMUS toward life." Bob says the Golden Rule means "Those who have the gold, rule." Think I'll chew on my Nylabone. And on this tangle-y CONUNDRUM. Too.

One writer my human quotes is M. Scott Peck. Who was a psychologist. And a Christian. Before he died he wrote. About *every*day human evil. In a yellow book. It's up on the book shelf. In our bedroom. I can see it. Third shelf from the top. In the psychology and philosophy section. Um hm. Meg CATEGORIZES books.

Dr. Peck wrote that those. Who harm others. Who make harmful choices. For their own pleasure. Profit. And gain. Are *evil*. Meg says that can include choices. About what we eat. I'd give him more wags. If he were vegan. And hadn't cheated. On his wife! Many times! Humph.

Hannah Arendt. Whoever she was. Had something to say. About evil. Too. Ask Meg. She reads this stuff. Hannah had an expression. The "banality of evil." Acts we consider normal. Committed by normal people. Who don't think. Choose forgetfulness. Concerning their choices and actions. That cause others. Including creatures. All life on the planet. Unnecessary harm and suffering. NORMALIZE evil. By making it COMMONPLACE. Familiar. Acceptable.

But Meg says. All cranked up. That humans connecting dots. Being aware. Of how they affect the rest of us is not a ready thought process. (Bear with me. I'll pass this along. Zippety zip.) For people living. In a violent nation. Like the United States. Where harm is an INTEGRAL part. Of the system. A nation that relies. On violence. Makes it feel okay. Serves it. At almost every meal. Hides it in plain sight. (Think humans wearing hunting and military camouflage designed. For killing. As fashion statements.) Anyhoo not often. She'll tell you. In this sort of numbed society. Do citizens consider. Honestly. How they cause harm. Hurt and destroy so many many beings. With their traditions. Insecurities. Entertainment. NORMS. Dress. Jobs. Food. GEOPOLITICAL games. That ignore the welfare of others. Especially those. Who are different. Who are not seen. And not human. Not a national habit to take responsibility. For all that.

"Too little thought given," Meg tells anyone who's still listening, "to these violent connections." "The US," says Jack, "is a nation that rarely tells hard truths about the suffering it inflicts and promotes." Meg adds, "With its history of cruelty and destruction. Built with cruelty. Demands cruelty to maintain its HEGEMONY with endless war. Profits from cruelty. Feeds off it." Like what Gandhi said, "Violence begins with a fork." Too little thought given. In America. "Where NOSTALGIA and MYTHS are preferred. To facts," says Meg. A nation that Martin Luther King called "the greatest purveyor of violence in the world."

Ooph! Ooph! Ooph! Anyhoo back. To the mice. Jack wasn't at the staff meeting. When the mice came up. Meg filled him in. She went on. And on. Hopping mad. Gets a little tedious. You know what I mean. By now. *Yadda yadda yadda.*

Meg spoke to the contractors hired to solve the "problem." About *not* killing them. They MANSPLAINED that mice carry diseases. She said, "Using that logic, we should kill humans for carrying over two hundred infectious diseases: STDs and FLU germs and AIDS and BLACK PIEDRA and MEASLES and SARS and PNEUMONIA and CHICKENPOX and GONORRHEA and HEPATITIS A B C D *and* E! And HERPES. Only six diseases carried by mice can infect humans. And *rarely*." Humph. Do the math! Folks. Mice are *not* the problem.

But so what. Meg points out that those. With the power rarely see themselves. As the issue. Dogs know this. On a very *personal* level. Think Michael Vick and dog fighting. Think puppy mills. Think dog-meat markets and dog-meat eating festivals. In Asia. Think research scientists. Who experiment on dogs. And other animals. Horrible experiments. Think men who use dogs. For sex! Think fur suppliers who rip off live dogs' skin. Think greyhounds hung to die. From trees. In Spain. Because they don't make money. For their owners. At the races. Think humans who cut dogs' vocal chords. So they won't bark. Because they're too lazy to help the dogs. Overcome their fear. Fear! That's why we bark! Folks. A lot of the time. Fear! And men and women. Who hit and kick their dogs. Leave them in *boiling*hot cars. Chain them outside in the cold and heat. Snow and rain. Who yank them around. By their necks. Think Iditarod competitors. And the grim existences. Of sled dogs. About military bomb-sniffing dogs. And what fate handed them. Humph. Humph. And HUMPH!

So here's how it goes down. For the mice. Snap traps. And sticky pads laid out. Desperate to escape. Mice chew *off* their *feet*. Stuck to the pads. Rats. Too. Just like wildlife in metal traps. "Ha ha." Meg says she can't get the principal's laugh. Out of her head. And the smirk. "Ha ha." Then they're trashed. After humans break their little necks. Humans. Who still leave food wrappers lying around. And crumbs. Grinds my stump. Twists my ears. Blisters my nose. Grates my teeth. Sizzles my whiskers!

"Use humane methods. Release the mice. Elsewhere," Meg snarled. At the guys the school district hired. She added, "If you don't stop putting out those snap traps and sticky pads, making the mice suffer, and killing them, Dori and I will write about *you*! In our book!" Now *there's a threat*! Um hm. They said, "They'll just come back into the school." Meg snorted, "So will the students. So will the teachers." Can only imagine what she really wanted to say. Bet she swallowed a SNIDE RETORT. Wanted to shout a four-letter word. Like *JERK*! Hurts my esophagus. When I hear that. Meg was REPRIMANDED in her year-end evaluation. For not being COLLEGIAL. For confronting contractors. Mind you! Who weren't colleagues! Just hired killers.

Dogs and humans have seventy-five COMMUNICABLE diseases. That's twelve-and-a-half times more than humans and mice! Um hm. Do people kill dogs? For having communicable diseases? Oh no. Well for rabies they do. So *why* mice? Humph. Makes me want to bite the humans. Who EXTERMINATE them. Tear holes in their clothes. Chew off their fingers. And toes. Exterminate! "That's what the Nazis did," Meg said. *Exterminate*! "Ha ha." Jews. Jehovah's Witnesses. Poles. Homosexuals. "Ha ha." Gypsies. Communists. The disabled. Blacks. The Nazis. Who signed the Concordat. With the Roman Catholic

Church. A treaty. Promising. That the Vatican would not OPPOSE the goals. Of the Nazi Party. The Church. That has the PEDOPHILE priest-molesting-children problem. "Ha ha."

This summer Meg and I will care. For Bob. Who's tip-pier than ever. While Nancy goes abroad. For three weeks. Bob gave her an anniversary trip. To Scotland. Meg said to Nancy, "This might be the last time you go there." Off and on. For sixty-two years Nancy has travelled. To Scotland.

Nancy loves all things Scottish. At twenty-two she saved every penny she could. Squeezed tooth-paste tubes. Flat. Turned inside out and remade. And mended her clothes. To afford her first airplane ticket. To Edinburgh. Where she met her pen pal Jean. After the Second World War. Meg has Jean's middle name. Margaret. Which is Greek! Um hm. Go figure. My name. Too. Dorothea! Greek.

"Like a true Scot," says Meg. "Nancy enjoys haggis." Just loves sheep and calf guts. From other mothers' babies. Mixed. With fat and organs. And oatmeal. Stuffed. Into a bag made from an animal's stomach! Meg begs her to buy only vegan haggis. Anyhoo every Wednesday night. Her mother goes Scottish dancing. Doesn't skip about anymore. Though. On her toes. When she dances the reels she shuffles. The younger men. Ever so nicely. Ask to be her partners.

Meg told Jack that the saddest years of her life lie ahead. For one she'll lose *me*. Ooph! Imagine thinking like Nancy. Thinking "My last trip." Makes me go *all* droopy and limp. At the joints. About being *old*old. Weak and leaky. Losing my mind. And my final ride. In the car to the clinic. Where Meg and Jack will kiss me. Rub my ears. And say, "Good bye, Dori. Thank you for the joy you brought. For making us better humans." Where my new veterinarian will put a port. Into my leg. And the needle. With the chemicals. That will kill me. I've heard

Meg and Jack talk. About how Kathryn*theveterinarian* did that. To Persis. Their first Boxer. Who had brain cancer. "We love you, Dori!" they'll say. As I slip away. In their arms. The last thing I'll feel will be tears. Hugs. I hope. And relief. Spike and Grace will die. Before *I* do. Something tells me. Ooph!

Been turning over. In my mind. The vegetable garden. And what will happen in it. While we're away. In Vermont. Noooo vegetable garden. For three weeks. While Meg takes care of her father. And the farmers' market. In Nancy's and Bob's town. Does *not* allow dogs to accompany their humans. While shopping. Humph.

But I'll play with Sophie. And maybe the black bear will visit. At night. The baby finches nesting. In the bird feeder. Though. Will be long gone. By the time we arrive. Meg and I will pick blueberries. And raspberries. Take walks down the lane. I'll chase Willie*the*cat. Maybe. He might be dead. Nancy says he has cancer. Of the jaw. After hearing the DIAGNOSIS she drove. Over a curb.

I hope the doe and her spotted fawns visit the yard. And snack on Nancy's apples. I'll bark at them. My friendliest *rrrrruff*. Maybe I'll try putting my head. On Bob's lap. Again. A bit of a risk. Meg will cook vegan meals. Nancy told him. Right in front of us! Mind you. Just before leaving. That while she's away. If he wants meat. Then he'll have to go out. For lunch. With his friends. For hot*dogs*. Ooph! Does Nancy know hot*dogs* cause cancer? Consider the animals' suffering?

Anyhoo I've never seen a hot*dog*. Pretty upsetting. People eating dogs. They do that. In Korea. Meg knows. And all through Asia. There the meat markets have piles. Of them. With sad faces. Crammed into stacked metal cages. Peeing and shitting. On one another. Their muzzles taped shut. No food. No water. Dogs watching other dogs die. While waiting. "In EERIE silence," says Meg, "to be killed." On a hike. In the mountains. Near Seoul. She saw a man burning fur. Off a dead dog. In the middle. Of the trail. With a blow torch. Before he ate it. Maybe hot*dogs* look like that! Makes me go all rubbery. And slack.

This year's half-planted vegetable garden looks pitiful! Only tomatoes and eggplants. Basil and arugula. I don't even *like* arugula. Peppers and cabbage. But *nooo* Brussels sprouts! *Nooo* broccoli! I'll have peppers. At least. And cabbage leaves. The farmer who sells organic plants. At the public market. Told my humans, "No Brussels sprouts." He had crop failure.

Meg says we've had apple crop failure. Too. Seventy-five percent. Of the apple crops. In our state died this spring. Because of the drought. And not enough bees. The bee colonies are in COLLAPSE. All over the world. My humans sign lots of save-the-bee petitions. Jack says "Three hundred and forty-one bee species are in decline." I haven't seen one honeybee this year. Not *one*! Only carpenter bees. Crawling in and out. Of Dr. Campbell's house.

Our garden needs bees. Most of the world's food plants need bees. Lots of scientists tell us PESTICIDES and HERBICIDES. Made by Monsanto. (Now Bayer.) Dow. DuPont and Syngenta. Used by AGRIBUSINESS. And small farms. On crops and gardens. And sprayed onto lawns. And golf courses kill the POLLINATORS. Kill bees and butterflies. *Whom* plants need to reproduce. Yup! I figured it out! The who*whom* SNAGGLE. Kill other BENEFICIAL insects. Too. Like lady bugs.

And here's what this dog doesn't get. Why poison the creatures. Who help you? "Life ends without bees and butterflies," Meg snapped. While I watched her weed. And then she went on. About how we don't have enough. Of them. To POLLINATE the world's fruits and vegetables. Grains and nuts. That means less broccoli. Fewer peppers and avocados. Not as much coffee. Beets. And alfalfa. And Brussels sprouts! Meg says CORPORATIONS make money destroying life. Humph! Humph! HUMPH! And *Grrrrr*!

Some students in Meg's *Sustainable Living* class insist. They will nev-erevernever have children. Well that's what they say. Now! They don't want their kids to suffer. From what's coming. Not enough food. And water. Temperatures too hot for humans. And animals. The UN warns. By 2050. Seventy-five percent. Of the world could face drought. Within fifty years half the planet will be UNINHABITABLE. Scientists predict. Meg says their calculations are usually way too OPTIMISTIC. And massive human die-offs. Yikes! Meg thinks all this will happen. Sooner. Much sooner! Because environmental collapse. And Global Warming are *speeding up*!

Too hot for more and more creatures. Becoming too hot. For dairy cows to go outside. And for plants. Life on this planet. Now disappearing at a rate of 30,000 species. A year! The physicist Stephen Hawking said. Before he died. That humans must leave the planet. *At once*! And colonize another. If they hope to survive. What a joke! They'll trash the next planet. Too. Take it from a dog. Who sniffs a lot of litter. And lawn chemicals. Who scratches her head. All the time. Over humans wrecking nature. On which life depends. No! I'm not scratching fleas. I simply don't get HOMO SAPIENS. *Are you all suicidal?*

Never before has Meg heard young people talk this way. Jack hasn't either. Other students think. That humans should speed up their own DEMISE. They think the clothes-wearing species is the can-cer. In the system. And doesn't deserve to live. That the environment would be better off. Without them. Doesn't need their kind. "Just get the whole thing over with," they say. "As soon as possible." Those are serious thoughts. For teenagers! Makes me want to roll over. And stick my legs straight up. Into the air. In DISMAY. Ooph! Ooph! Ooph! Such PESSIMISM. In young people. But something deep down tells me they're right. After all. It's official. We're in the SIXTH MASS EXTINCTION. Yup! Humans have really messed things up! For everyone.

Meg asked Sam what his friends have to say. About environmental collapse. They're in their twenties. He told his mother. That his friends "don't give a damn." Ooph! Ooph! Ooph! Too busy playing *Starcraft* and *League of Legends*. *Halo II*. *Minecraft*. And *America's Army*. A killing game! Folks. With 9.7 million registered users. Developed by the U.S. military. Meg bets they all eat animals. Too. And drink their fluids. Um hm.

Nature feels peculiar. Now we have super weeds. In our yard. Huge! And hard to pull out. Believe me. My humans have tried. Great big beetles. Drought. With violent rain storms. That wash away roads. Every now and then. A video Meg watched. On her computer. Shows the ice caps almost gone. From the North and South Poles. Because the planet's hotter. Growing hotter. That means the polar bears will drown. If they're not killed first. By rich people. Who hunt them. For "fun" and fur. And what about the penguins? They'll commit suicide. Did you know penguins do that. When they are stressed. And desperate?

Melting ice caps release lots. Of methane. More than scientists ever imagined possible. And methane is that greenhouse gas. That's worse than CO_2. But methane doesn't just get released. From melting ice caps. Folks. In the U.S. methane from livestock and natural gas. Are almost equal. Add in methane from the rest of the world's meat and gas production. You get where I'm going! Jack says the president of the Institute of Governance & Sustainable Developments warns us: "Methane is the blowtorch that is cooking us today." Crikey!

Meg wants to know. About this stuff. (She says non-stop, "Jack, listen to *this*!") That oceans grow warmer. And warmer. Absorbing more and more CO_2. With less and less oxygen. The oceans' animals can't breathe. And suffocate. The water conveyor belts. That STABILIZE ocean temperatures. And SALINITY. Have slowed down. Now the oceans are dying. And expanding. As they heat up. Flooding coastlines. Crop lands poisoned by salt water. Ooph! Meg says we'll have DIASPORAS. Thousands and millions. Of humans and animals. Fleeing floods. Then there are the wildfires. Wilder. And bigger. And more and more of them. Millions. And millions of acres. From outer space. Astronauts can see the planet going up. In smoke. And thousands of homes. Torched. Every summer. Now. Where do dogs go? And wild creatures? And bugs? The ones. Who don't become charred and crispy. When their places COMBUST. The ones. Who don't go up in flames. And turn to ashes.

What doesn't burn. Humans find other ways to do in. Finish off. Dig up. Suck out. Pollute. Meg huffs when she talks. About this. And cut down. Like twenty-five percent. Of the Amazon Rainforest. At a rate of one and a half acres. Every second. Just like that! Each day. Two hundred thousand acres destroyed. The "lungs of the planet!" Folks. That helps SEQUESTER the greenhouse gas CO_2. And cools Earth. Most of the Amazon destruction. Up to ninety-one percent. Of the clearing. For animal agriculture. Like INTENSIVE beef-cattle farming. In Asia. Too. Rainforests. Wiped out. For palm oil plantations. At the rate of forty football fields every minute. Creatures losing their forest homes. Where can they go? To survive?

Meg rants. On the phone. With Nancy. And her sister Elizabeth. And brother James. With Ellie. And Sam. You get the idea! And with guests. During dinners. But not with the sister. Who says Global Warming is a HOAX! Ooph! I wish it were. Kind of a nice thought. Though. No change required. No extra effort and responsibility called for! And not with her youngest brother. Who says he doesn't want any negative news.

Everything will be much worse. By the time you read this. Already there are water wars. More than half the people. On the planet hungry. And starving. Not enough food. Due to drought. And most of the world's farmland being used. For mono crops. For farmed-animal food. A Cornell professor of ECOLOGY says the 'U.S. can feed 800 million people with the grain grown to feed livestock. Each year. In the United States. Alone.'

My humans wonder. What more they can do? Other than buy second-hand. And eat a whole-foods plant-based diet? Eat only what's in season. Grow vegetables. Join co-operatives. Avoid plastic. That's a tough one. Push back against the meat and dairy. And egg and fishing industries. And corporations. That kill the planet. And creatures. With pesticides and herbicides. With pollution and greenhouse gases. And toxic waste. They protest. Sign petitions. Vote. Boycott. Write letters to politicians and newspapers. Shop as little as possible. And carefully. Recycle. Purchase electricity gen-erated by wind. And sun. They read articles and books. To learn everything they can. Spread the word about farmed-animal and wildlife genocides. You know the numbers by now! One hundred fifty billion farmed animals slaughtered every year and trillions of water animals. Ninety percent of all large ocean fish. Dead. As much as eighty-three percent of all wildlife. Gone. Murdered by humans. PANTOPIC deaths of insects. Too. About Global Warming and the Sixth Mass Extinction. The biggest one since the dinosaurs died. Caused by human activity. An extinction not caused. By *dogs*! Mind you. Not by ants and elephants. Rabbits and pangolins. Couldn't be pangolins. They're being slaughtered. Into OBLIVION. For Chinese medicine. Not caused by sharks. Who are caught. Fins cut off. For soup. Then they're thrown back. Amputated. Into the water. Can't swim. So they suffocate and die. Ooph! Splits my whiskers. Slices my paws! Meg and Jack could buy an electric car!

They discuss this at breakfast. At dinner. In bed. At night. But re-ally I don't want to hear. Any of it. I just want to play. With Grace and Spike. And lie in the grass. (So what if it's brown and scratchy. From no rain. And gives me a *red*rash. On my stomach. Anything's better than knowing. The *awful*truth.) And chew. On a dandelion root. I mean tell me. What can *one* dog do?

What can I do? To help our planet? That's *outofsorts*. Too *too*hot. And strange. Because as Meg says, "Humans haven't tried hard enough. To do the least harm." Now we have intense storms. Increasing DESERTIFICATION. Dying oceans. Melting polar ice caps. Melting faster than ever imagined. Wild plants and animals going extinct. At the rate of three species every hour. Diseases spreading. Blood flowing. From fishing trawlers. Slaughterhouses. And wars for dwindling re-sources. More and more disturbing events. Like this one! I saw with my own eyes! On a walk. A little old man. With a white beard. Um hm. Wearing a blue jacket and red hat. In ninety-nine degree weather! Limp on his back. In the grass.

I sniffed. *Nuph nuph nuph.* Meg said, "Dori. He's a garden gnome." *Nuph nuph nuph.* A garden gnome? Humph! Why wasn't he in a garden? That alone tells me things are out-of-whack. More to the point. Why don't *we* have a garden gnome. In *our* vegetable garden? Maybe he's the garden gnome. Who no longer roams. All around the world. Taking a well-deserved nap. Or was he fried? I couldn't tell. At the side of the road. Overdressed. Dead from *extreme heat*!

Yes*siree*! The world's gone BERZERK! Week before last we saw a *green* man! Riding a bicycle. He had hairy green arms. I kid you not! And really really hairy green legs. Ooph! Pumping up and down. Up and down. As fast as he could go. We stood on the sidewalk. Couldn't move. RIVETED. Watching him ride toward us. And he wore a yellow football helmet. Sprouting long ANTENNAE. With yellow tennis balls. On their tips. He peered at me. As he rode by. Squinted through thick glasses. "Hello," he said. In a deep voice. We stared. Stunned. Who was he? Meg wondered whether he's another INVASIVE SPECIES. Come north. Fleeing rising temperatures.

Environmental scientists say more and more extreme PHENOMENA are rushing. At us. Head long. A TSUNAMI of disturbing events. How would those scientists explain. If they knew. The garden gnome. Lying by the curb. Wearing a hat and coat. In asphalt-melting weather? The green man on a bicycle? And the vegan woman. Who talks. With a plant-eating dog. About this stuff? A dog who's writing. To you!

This afternoon Jack came home. With collards. Cauliflower. Rosemary plants. And Brussels sprouts! He found Brussels sprouts! For the vegetable garden. Later this summer Meg will pickle crunchy cauliflower. With ginger. Pepper corns. Onions and carrots. And fill jars. With chutney. Of unripe green tomatoes. Raisins. And bruised apples. She'll use the rosemary. In soups. And in her avocado-chocolate mousse. That she'll make tomorrow. After she weeds. And tucks the new plants. Into the warm soil. Patting it firm. I'll watch from the lawn. And chew a stick. Maybe she'll play ball. With me and Spike. After she's done. Grace will bark. On the sidelines.

It's taken three weeks. Longer than usual. But finally Meg cleaned the big screened summer porch. And set it up. Says she's tired of the routine. Every year she mixes vinegar and environmentally-friendly cruelty-free plant-based dish detergent. The same stuff she uses on us. Into a bucket of hot water. No commercial petroleum-based cleaning agents. Not in our house. *No*siree! Then she vacuums the floor-to-ceiling screens. Inside and out. Washes them. Scrubs the flagstones. On her hands and knees. Scrubs the wood picnic table. And benches. Vacuums the wicker chairs. Washes windows overlooking the porch. Wipes cobwebs. From the corners. Polishes glass globes. For the ceiling lights. And screws them back. Into place. Brings chair cushions. Out of storage. At last she spreads a clean yellow sun-faded India-print table cloth. Over the picnic table. And lays down a large cotton rug. For Spike's and Gracie's naps. And mine.

Our family spends quiet evenings. On the porch. Until dark settles. Into the neighborhood. When cicadas end their scratchy tunes. Birds grow silent. And fireflies turn off their lights. Then it's time. For bed.

Wag*wag*wag. *Phisst!* Ellie's home from Utah. Where she helps troubled teenagers. Home for a visit. In September she'll move back. Here. And live with us. She first went to the Four Corners. Years ago. Sent there. By her dad and Meg. Hoping she'd get it together. Ellie broke laws. Not just once. Not twice. Nope. More than that. The therapist said, "I'll work with your daughter, only *after* she goes through an implosion program." That's for *wild*kids! Folks. So they had her "kidnapped." In the early morning. By two psychologists. And flown. To a ranch. In the middle of nowhere. There she lived. In a tent. Rubbed sticks together. Built fires. To keep herself warm. Through the cold nights.

Ellie did things dogs never get to do. *Bad*ass choices! Um hm. Even ran away. From home. Gone for weeks. Wild! And free! Meg helped the state police find her. Under a pile of dirty clothes. In a college dorm. Most dogs never have adventures. On the loose. Go anywhere and do what they want. Some escape. Have ESCAPADES. But I don't think I'll have the chance. Ever! That's why I hang around. When Meg tells *Ellie*stories.

Meg and Jack and Ellie's dad call those seven years the "*hell*years." The kid didn't stop. At lying and drinking. Stealing and drugs. Oh no. She went all out. And told Meg. That having her mother. As her English teacher *ruined her life*! Now that's rich. Really *really*rich. She would've had her rump bitten. If she'd been my daughter. And said that to me. Humph! *Biiiitten*! Her nose chewed. Her elbows gnawed. Tail twisted. And her ears pulled. Until she yelped. Um hm.

But I'll never be a mother. I could have nursed ten puppies. All at once. Ten! If Meg and Jack hadn't signed the paper. Promising I would be spayed. A condition. Of my adoption. And then paid Kathryn*the*veterinarian. To remove *my* uterus. Maybe someday my humans will adopt. A rescued puppy. To be mine. Like they adopted me. And Spike and Grace. Maggie*the*cockatiel. And Ellie and Sam. Meg says everyone. In our family. Is second- and third-hand. Recycled. Re-loved. Including Meg and Jack.

Learned the hard way. Ellie went to jail. After she stood. In an orange jumpsuit and handcuffs. And ankle chains. Before the judge. To receive her sentence. Meg had to buy her white cotton underpants. No thongs allowed. In jail. *No*siree. Not even the zesty red ones. With fur and lace. And hearts. She'd left lying. On the laundry floor. Only *white cotton underpants*. That go all the way up. To your waist. Um hm. Um hm.

Meg never said whether she felt a moment. Of sweet revenge. As she handed her daughter white cotton underpants. Which Meg then wore. After Ellie got out of jail. And went back to her thongs. No sense throwing away perfectly good underwear. Meg saves our ripped up and gutted dog toys. Too. All the legs and heads. And wings. We pulled. Off the mail carrier and duck. Fox. And cat. We have a *basket*full. Of parts. That we chew on. Anyhoo Meg tossed the last worn-out pair. Of underpants. Into the trash. Soon after I arrived. By then Ellie was long on the mend.

Odd part. Now Meg *thanks* her daughter! For those awful years. *Thanks* her! I hear her. Um hm. Says the experience helps her understand. So much better. Her students' poor choices. And their parents' frustrations. Heartbreak. And anger. Now my human understands. That anger is the flip side. Of fear. Meg and Jack say that Spike and Grace. And I help them. Too. We and Ellie. And Sam as well. Teach them *compassion*. Yup! And patience. And do you know what else makes my stump wag*wag*wag? My humans' daughter grew up. Ever so kind and thoughtful. And she's a hoot! Makes my humans laugh. *Phisst!* She's my heroine. *Bounce bounce bounce!* Just hit a "bumpy patch." As Nancy says.

And get this! The implosion program. In Utah. Invited her b*a*ck! To work as a counselor! That's like an aggressive dog. Becoming a child's therapy companion. For five years she's taught horsemanship there. A fine rider. She has a pink lasso. *Yessiree!* But she rode with the cowboys. To round up the cattle. And herd them. Into winter pastures. To be slaughtered. For meat. *Grrrrr!* Makes me want to piss on their *pointy*leather cowboy boots. Really *soak* them!

Ellie will drive home. More than two thousand miles. To Upstate New York. In a few weeks. Saddest part. She can't bring Pony. Her horse. Whom she saved. From being shot. In the head. She can't bring her dogs. Either. The two who weren't killed. By a neighbor. She hopes she can find them loving families. Ellie will live with us. For awhile. And be *my* own special friend. Because it looks like I won't see Kenneth. Again. Nope! Kenneth wanted to come. To our house. For a vegan dinner. So he set a date with Meg and Jack. They cooked and cleaned. Cleaned and cooked. But Kenneth never showed up.

A sad sad day today. Nancy took Willie*the*cat. To the clinic. His cancer could not be treated. And he had grown so very very frail. From not eating. Became thin. As thread. And some of his striped gray fur. Turned *orange*! Meg says from MALNUTRITION. Nancy held him. While the vet put the needle. Into his little gray-and- black-striped twig of a leg. He went limp. Eleven years old. He'd always walked. With his tail held high. How I'd walk. If I had *mine*.

Nancy met Willie*the*kitten. In a shelter. He came over and sat. By her side. Looked up. And purred. That was that. Nancy will sprinkle his ashes. In her garden. Maybe I'll be able to smell him. Just a whiff. Among the phlox and lilies. I'll nuph nuph nuph. Ever so hard. Among the lilacs. And in the yellow ligularia. Too. Nancy says Sophie looks everywhere. For Willie. I'll miss watching him. Through the sliding glass door. To the deck. He would sit. On one side. And I on the other. Nose to the glass. Wanting to chase him. Ever so much.

And this afternoon Kathryn*the*veterinarian called Meg. With Spike's test results. "Spike has cancer," she said. *Third* time. First time since becoming vegan. Humph. Meg says an animal-free diet helps prevent cancer. But then maybe the growth began. Before Meg changed our meals. Spike will have an operation. At the end of the week. Kathryn says his PROGNOSIS looks good. Though. A tiny lump. Maybe eating plants slowed down the cancer? Anyhoo an unhappy day.

Spike came home. From the animal hospital. All woozy. Couldn't walk. In a straight line. Drooling from anesthesia. And pain killers. Kathryn stapled his side together. Six inches of staples. In a few days we'll know. Whether Spike has Stage One or Two or Three cancer. Kathryn will un-staple Spike. In twelve days. Meg warned me, "Dori, do *not* lick Spike's INCISION." Ooph! But I think I should. Um hm. When it itches. Because Spike's tongue can't reach. Where Kathryn sliced him open.

A happy day today. Cool. Not so humid. I poked around the yard. Lay in the sun. And barked. At the yappy little Shih tzus. On the other side. Of the crooked stockade fence. That offends Meg's aesthetic sensibilities. Kathryn*the*veterinarian left a message. On the answering machine. While I sniffed here. And there. Meg ran onto the porch. After she listened. And called to Jack, "Spike had Stage One cancer. And Kathryn removed it all!" *Phisst*! Spikey's fine!

Then I watched a hummingbird hover in the garden. And *whirrrrr* through the Russian sage and the orange lilies. And the pale purple hostas. Where a Monarch Butterfly flitted. Arugula crowds the collards. Ooph! Too much arugula. Blossoms cover the eggplants and pepper plants. And the basil and spearmint have grown bushy. Brown edges on leaves. From the drought. Even though Jack waters. Every day.

Two cardinals flew in and out. In and out. Of the Rose of Sharon tree. Carrying twigs. And chased off pesky wrens. Meg says, "Expect babies, soon. Before Ellie comes home from Utah." She wishes her daughter could bring her animal family. With her. But we have no room.

I think Ellie will cry buckets. As she drives away. From her caramel coon hound. Her gray and white husky. And her sandy mare. Who will stay behind. In the small rough town in the rocky-red West. Meg grows quiet. Thinking about Pony. And the dogs. About their confusion and anxiety. And grief. No one likes being left behind. Abandoned. By those whom you trusted. For love and protection.

A soft day in Vermont. Misty rain. Reminds me. Of my sisters and brothers. Sniffing and licking under my ears. A quiet day. Sophie didn't want to tumble. And chase. Bob said she worries. Without Nancy. Who's gone to Scotland. And misses Willie*the*cat. I miss Willie. As well. Out of habit I looked for him. In Nancy's painting studio. Where he perched on the stairs. To the loft. His food and water dishes gone. From the fifth step up. And missing. The safety gate. That stopped Sophie and me. From chasing him. The carved wood box. With his ashes. Sits on the entryway table. Nancy didn't have time. To sprinkle him. In the garden. Before she left.

Meg and I walked down to the end. Of the lane. At sunrise. To the dirt road. Through the woods and fields. To the far meadow. Where we met a black cow. A chestnut calf. Another the color of wicker. And a black and white new-born covered with flies. The calf's nose *ten* times the size of *mine*! We stood face to face. The chestnut calf and I. She licked me. My fur stood up. In a ridge. All down my back. Um hm. Frogs in the pond croaked. *Grunk grunk. Grunk grunk.* On the return. In a high field stood the mahogany horse. Further on two crows flew up. From the road. Into a sugar maple. *Caw caw*!

After my breakfast. Of vegan kibble and kidney beans. Mashed yams. And oat milk. Meg and I drove. To The Danowitz. She bought birdseed. A glass jug. And dental floss. Then on to the farm stand. For ears of corn. Salad greens. And two red tomatoes.

Meg washed bathrooms. Dusted and vacuumed. Sophie let me snooze. In her dog bed. Then we picked Nancy's blueberries. For dessert. And bright pink phlox. To toss onto the dinner salad. I nosed IRIDESCENT Japanese beetles. Piled on one another. Eating the raspberry leaves. Into lace. I raced. Around the yard. Circled the apple tree and the blueberry patch. And the apple tree. Again! Round and around. Took a late afternoon nap. With Meg.

At dawn we walk. Sun on the horizon. Among maple trees and pine. Oak. Birch and beech. Skirt high meadows. Above the river valley. That separates Vermont and New Hampshire. We take dirt roads between old stone walls. Covered in gray-green lichen. Gauzes spun by spiders. Strung. With water beads stretch. Between blades of grass. Among purple clover and goldenrod. Queen Anne's lace. And thistles. "The national flower of Scotland," says Meg.

This morning as we do each day. We visited the cow. And the calves. "Hello," Meg called. They'd moved. To the lower pasture. Where it meets the cool dark woods. Cattle! Oh cattle! *Bounce bounce*

bounce! I went all silly. Nipped Meg's fingers. Bounced and pranced. Tugged on my leash and laughed. *Phisst*! Meg taped. Onto the metal gate a plastic bag. With a letter. To the farmer. Urging him not to slaughter them. She included the telephone number. Of a nearby farmed-animal sanctuary.

We climbed back up the hill. Toward Bob's and Nancy's. And Sophie's house. A doe leapt. Across the road. Into the mown meadow. Where the farmer will bale hay. This afternoon. She met another. They frisked lippity lippity. To the woods. Wag*wag*.

"Here, in Vermont," Meg says, "it's easy to forget our troubled world. To ignore our country's endless IMPERIALIST wars that overturn and take lives and poison foreign countries for eternity with DEPLETED URANIUM. Easy to not think about corporations devouring the planet. Destroying us and the animals. To forget human greed and narcissism. Forget human HUBRIS. And the myths and lies that people live by, willingly. That ruin our present and future, forever." I know all this sounds too DOUR. For a young dog to repeat. But that's what happens. When you hang around someone. Who reads serious books. Writes. Protests. And frets. About the state of the world. Her children's futures. About the fate of animals. At the hands of humans. Um hm. Um hm. About *me*! And Spike and Grace. About two-legged friends and family. But I must pass this stuff along. Bark. Yelp. Howl. Snarl. Growl. Insist you listen. Before it's too late. Which it almost is.

Tomorrow. We drive to Burlington. Meg says that we'll join the RESISTANCE. Against the tar-sands pipeline. That energy corporations want to build. Through Vermont and New Hampshire. From Canada. But what does this have to do. With me? I ask you.

"Tar sands yield dirty oil," Meg explains. To anyone who asks. "And mining and drilling. For fossil fuels. And burning them. Poison the land and water. The air. Heat it all up, too. Along with farming animals for food, which requires using vast quantities of non-renewable energy." Um Hm. Killing all life. Except perhaps bacteria. Mosquitoes.

Viruses and mushrooms. Now we have the hottest summer. On record. Every year hotter. Than the one before. And the pipeline has everything to do. With this environmental crisis. *And* with me! A *vegan*dog. *Everything*. Meg insists we must learn to see how it *all* connects. To huge corporations. To human arrogance. To the food we eat!

Let me and Meg remind you. Producing meat and dairy uses billions of gallons. Of fossil fuels. "Vegans," Meg points out, "help reduce fossil fuel use. *A lot*! And those, who eat UNPROCESSED plants, help the most." Yeah yeah yeah! I can guess the rest! The more unprocessed whole-plant foods humans and dogs consume. Then the more nutrients they INGEST. And the less fossil fuel burned. If we all ate plants. Only. There'd be no need. For pipelines. To carry dirty oil. From humongous open. Black. Sticky DOOMSDAY pits. Like the Alberta Tar Sands. And Athabasca oil sands. In Canada. Meg showed me and Jack pictures.

She'll tell anyone who'll listen. Anyone who's forced to listen! Like yours truly! That animal-based foods require tons more fossil fuels. Twenty-five times more. Than plant-based foods. For each pound produced. And tons more water. To produce one KILOGRAM of animal protein takes one hundred times more water. Than producing an equal weight of plant protein. And Meg says again. And again. Raising animals. For human consumption is *THE* biggest source. Of greenhouse gasses. That cause Global Warming. And climate change. Driving the Sixth Mass Extinction. She read somewhere "livestock production has the heaviest carbon footprint of any of the parts of our food chain." Why?

Ah hem. I need to lie down for this. Put my head. On my paws. Close my eyes. I feel one coming. A DIATRIBE. "Fossil fuels are used to warehouse animals on small farms and on huge automated factory farms. For sucking out animal secretions. For planting and harvesting crops. For animal feed. Like GMO soy and corn planted and harvested with farm equipment run on fossil fuels. Also used to operate equipment. To water crops. And spray pesticides and herbicides and fertilizers made from petrochemicals. Used to transport farmed animals. To operate slaughterhouses. And processing and bottling plants. To refrigerate animal flesh and fluids. Used for assembly lines to cook and pasteurize and package. For plastic packaging made from oil and plastic containers for dairy. Transport animal products in refrigerated trucks. To stores heated and lit with energy from fossil fuels. For energy to run the pharmaceutical corporations and manufacturers and distribution systems for this industry. Big pharma that sells eighty percent of all antibiotics made in the U. S. to animal agriculture. That then go into people. When they eat the animals. An industry that becomes even wealthier off people sickened by meat and dairy and eggs and fish. That can cause heart disease. And cancer. That is only five to ten percent genetic! Um hm. Alzheimer's. Arthritis. GERD. Lupus and diabetes. Connect the dots. Fossil fuels to farmed animals to big pharma," says Meg. Ooph! And humph! Humph! And ooph!

"That's a lot of fossil fuel." Meg adds. "That produces a lot of CO_2. In a system that also ends up creating a lot of methane from those farmed animals. And from their pee and feces. And from manufacturing waste, which off-gasses methane in landfills." Methane! Yup. Like my human explains. Over and over. That further warms the atmosphere. And oceans.

Whenever I cock my head. And look BEFUDDLED. And move the black spots. Above my eyes. Up and down. Because I only *sort*of understand these things. I get a lecture. You know the drill by now. And *you* end up reading it. Here. In this book. All fiery and *long*winded. And INDIGNANT. Ooph! But I think it's too important. For Meg not to write down. For me. What I hear her say. For you to read. So you can draw lines from everything. To everything. Which Meg and Jack didn't do. For most of their lives. Um hm. And they still knock themselves for that. For all the harm they've done. Especially to animals. Who can't protect themselves. From humans. And to the planet.

Anyhoo about the big protest. In Burlington. Tomorrow. We'll join a "human oil spill." Supposed to wear black. But I'm a white dog. Meg looked for a small black T-shirt. For me. At The Danowitz. But then she thought it would be *too*hot. To wear over a fur coat. On a summer day. And they weren't organic. Ooph! Meg said I could be a white Styrofoam cup. That doesn't BIODEGRADE. And gives people cancer. Bobbing along. In the big human oil spill.

Environmentalist Bill McKibben. Who told Meg he's *not* vegan. Yup! Will speak. Meg wants to know. How can he be an environmentalist. And *not* be vegan. She used to email him. From time to time. And asked, "Are you vegan, yet?" He stopped answering "no." Long ago. He has important things to say. Though. About CO_2. Even if he doesn't mention methane. And the other dangerous greenhouse gases. From farming animals. For food. Meg has a theory. Yup! Another one. About his OMISSIONS. Um hm.

Early this morning we went for our daily walk. Before the long drive north to protest. The sun struggled to shine. Through dense mist. A crow cawed. Once. Frogs had nothing to say. No breeze. Heavy air. Damp from last night's rain. No mahogany horse. On the hill.

As we turned the bend. Onto the dirt road. Through the high meadow. We saw TAWNY fur. In the ditch. A fawn. With small velvet buds. His first antlers. Lay on his side. Head back. Dead. Tail and haunches ripped off. A WARY doe watched nearby.

We stopped. Shocked. Meg asked, "Could she be looking for her child? Could he be the spotted fawn who slept on the lawn by Nancy's studio?" The doe flashed her tail. Crossed the road to the meadow. And back again. Through the tall grass. At her side. Two yearlings kicked up their heels.

We left behind dark clouds. As we drove north. To the tar-sands pipeline protest. I rested my chin. On the back of the seat. And watched the world DWINDLE. Green hills. Green fields. Green mountains. Meg says Vermont lives up to its French name.

Along the highway electronic signs flashed messages. Meg read them aloud. One flashed '50 deaths on VT highways this year.' Ooph! That number is *so* wrong. Did anyone count the deer and possums. Raccoons and skunks and bears. Moose. Foxes. Birds. Chipmunks.

Squirrels and coyotes. Wolves. Cats. Dogs. Flies. Butterflies. Mosquitoes and moths. The frogs and toads. Bobcats and fishers. Fleas. Caterpillars. Ants. Snakes and worms. Rabbits. Woodchucks. Porcupines and spiders? Oh no. They did not. A lot more of us creatures die. On the roads than humans. Don't we count? Humph. Humph. HUMPH! Maybe if we did count. And *were* counted. The planet wouldn't be going. To wrack and ruin. Um hm. Another thing to think about.

Before the march people gathered. At City Hall. From New England. Canada. And New York! *Yes*siree! Meg and Dori from New York! With banners and signs. And guitars. Whistles. Trombones. Drums. And pans for banging. And dogs. Every size and color. Even another white Boxer puppy. Just like me! Ooph! *I*. We had a *little* rumpus. As he was very young. And I am now two! With muscles. Um hm. Women and children asked to pat me. But I backed. Into Meg. Too many hands. In my face. Smelling of stinky lotion and steering wheels. And McMuffins. There were speeches. That we couldn't hear. And then we walked. In the streets. And walked. Through the city. Some protestors danced. Led by a noisy band. Of gray-haired women and men. Wearing red pajamas.

The crowd grew bigger. Along the way. And bigger. Until it stopped. In front. Of a hotel. Where New England governors and Canadian politicians discussed the pipeline. People waved signs. Chanted. "Come out! Come out! We have something to talk about!" No one appeared. Meg gave me a bowl of water.

At the park. Overlooking Lake Champlain. We sat. On cool grass. In the shade of an oak tree. Rested. And waited. For Bill McKibben to speak. A little girl rubbed me. Under my chin. And cooed. In that annoying way so many girls and women do. All high-pitched and squeaky. Baby talk. Hurts a dog's ears. Ooph! And our pride. Um hm.

By now the day had grown late. And we had a long drive ahead. Back. To Bob's and Nancy's. And Sophie's home. So we returned to the car. Meg didn't seem concerned we'd miss McKibben's speech. She'd read his book *Eaarth*. I'd considered chewing it up. Yup! It sits in a pile. Of books. On a blue metal table. A kind of modern-looking thing. By her side of the bed. Where she read his article *Global Warming's Terrifying New Math*. I'm sure she knew. What he would say. To the protesters. Who were pepper sprayed. After we left. And shot. With rubber bullets. By the police. And that he'd leave out. As he has in the past. The impact. On the environment. Of farmed animals. Producing CO_2. Methane. And nitrous oxide. Farming animals and all that involves. Being one of the biggest. If not the biggest producers of greenhouse gases.

Meg wondered could it be. This is her theory. That environmental organizations accept money. From the RUTHLESS meat and dairy industries? "If that's true," she said to Jack. When she called him later that night, "then maybe that's why McKibben doesn't share all the facts. About greenhouse gases from animal agriculture and global warming. Because he and they don't want to INFURIATE the companies and lobbyists making up the huge systems that use animals. Those environmental groups don't want to bite the hands. That feed them." *Ha*! I get *that* expression! "Because they'll get bitten back," she added.

This idea. Of possible unethical ENTANGLEMENTS. Came to her. After watching a documentary. "Is this the deal?" she asks. "Environmental non-profits accept meat and dairy companies' sponsorships and don't expose them in return. Kind of like The American Diabetes Association, Susan G Komen and American Heart Association. In the film they're shown to be sponsored by meat and dairy companies. Then, on their websites, in recipes for healthy eating, those non-profits feature animal foods that cause the deadly diseases they claim they're trying to cure. Have environmental non-profits made deals with the devil, too?" She reminded me. As if I need reminding, "Dots, Dori. Remember the dots! Connect them." Then she made this ANALOGY. "Kind of like pimps," Meg said, "getting 'their girls' addicted to drugs." Yup! Just a theory.

Anyhoo I'm sure she would tell me. On the drive home. That McKibben would speak. About this 'past May being the warmest May. On record. For the Northern Hemisphere. The 327th consecutive month. In which the temperature. Of the entire globe. Exceeded the twentieth-century average. And that the odds of that occurring.

By simple chance is a number considerably larger. Than the number of stars in the universe.' Ooph!

I fell asleep. Pooped after parading around. For two hours! In the bright sun. On hot asphalt. Made from fossil fuels! And trying to imagine the UNIVERSE. Filled with billions of stars. Trying to understand. All the numbers. That explain how hot the planet has become. How much hotter it grows. Every year. *Even as the Sun cools down*! But really a dog doesn't need math to know temperatures are rising. Only a fur coat. Yup!

And maybe. Just maybe. Humans would get with the program. And try to stop this insanity a lot faster. Stop doing things. That make the planet UNINHABITABLE. Like eating animals and their fluids. If they all had to wear fake fur coats. During the summer. And really suffer. Feel a little bit. Of what's coming. But there's a problem with that. SYNTHETIC fur's made from oil. So maybe. If they all wore fleeces. In the heat. Made from recycled plastic soda bottles. Then they might change their ways. In the wag of a tail! Um hm. But fleeces pollute water. With tiny bits of plastic. So does fake fur. Ooph! When washed.

Really got to think solutions through. Glad my coat comes. With the package. I don't have to struggle. With what's ethical to wear. And it's made from plants! Organic vegan kibble. And vegetable-fruit smoothies! *Phisst*!

After dinner with Bob. I walked. By Meg's side. Slowly. She carried a large bouquet. Of flowers. From Nancy's gardens. To where the yearling died. In a pool of blood. On the grass and ferns. By the old tumbled-down stone wall. But he had been removed. By *whom*? We'll never know. Ooph! Got the *whom* right. Again! Don't have to think. About grammar that much. Anymore. Writing a book. With Meg kind of polishes up a dog.

She placed the flowers. On the ground. Flies swarmed the sticky BURGUNDY grass. A lone robin sang with the crickets. A wild turkey floated down. Wings outspread. Onto a dead tree's overhanging branch. Laid down the bundle of orange lilies and yellow ligularia. Fuschia. White phlox. Bright pink coreopsis and red bee balm. "Good bye, Fawn," Meg said. To the empty spot. We stood silent. Robin finished her song. Turkey lifted herself from the branch. And flew to the far edge. Of the meadow.

We headed home. In the dusk. Spent. I didn't feel like sniffing. Just trotted along. Soon the full moon would rise. And brighten the shadowy woods. From where the screech owl calls.

Here in Vermont. I miss Spike. And Grace. And Maggie*the*cockatiel's songs. And curling up against Jack. While he reads. I miss running in and out. I do. My humans leave the doors open. To the porch. And back yard. Spring. Summer. And Fall. We come and go. As we please. So do the bugs. I miss rumpuses with Spike cheered on. By Grace. And tucking in. Among my family of five. On *our* bed. After quiet evenings. On the porch. I miss our vegetable garden.

Meg says that just about this time. Last year. I started in. On the garden. Only she didn't know. That I was the one. Enjoying it. First she saw the half-eaten cabbages. Then collard leaves went missing. Peppers. And broccoli. "Rabbits?" Meg asked Jack. The arugula remained untouched. "Not rabbits," Meg decided.

Leaves and stems. And chewed vegetables. Strewn about the back yard. Gave me away. I'd hop the fence. Bite off a pepper. Take a few chunks. From a cabbage plant. A collard leaf. Or two. Then hop out. Carrying the goods. And share the harvest. With my crew. Who stood by the fence. Eyeing Brussels sprouts. As if to say, "Could you bring us some of those, too? Please!" We three had picnics. On the lawn. Flower gardens in bloom. Cicadas sawing tunes. Blue skies. Meg explained the word "picnic" comes from the French *piquer*. Which means "to pick."

Jack caught me. First. Um hm. Standing. In the garden. With a Brussels sprout stalk. In my mouth. Ooph! Passed off my best *hi-pal-this-isn't-what-you-think* look. "Dorioutofthere," he said. So out I hopped. Wagwagwag. I *am* a wag! Jack never raises his voice. He's calm. And like I said *very*tall. It's the *very*tall part. And his deep voice. That MOTIVATE me. And his students. Too. And his law clients.

He and I went through this routine. Every so often. Last summer. Um hm. Meg and I went through it. As well. Because I kept hopping the fence. Couldn't help myself. "Dorioutofthere." Wag *wag*. Grace and Spike never entered the garden. Which began looking ratty. Then RANSACKED.

Actually I think Meg and Jack were proud. Of me! After all. Only a real *vegan*dog. Or a starving one. Would eat. With a boost. From you know who! Ooph! *Whom*! A whole vegetable garden. Except for the peppery arugula. Um hm. Um hm. Meg told me I'd helped save the planet. And Grace and Spike. Too. "You know, Dori," she said, "The United Nations." Whatever *that* is. "In 2010 called on everyone. The entire world population. To go vegan, or it's *THE END*." Get it? Folks. Curtains! For humans. And animals. Insects and plants.

Think I've caught on! *Prance prance prance*! If we all stop finding excuses. Eat only fruits and vegetables. Nuts and grains. Then everyone. Everywhere. Could have enough food. And be healthy. We'd use less fossil fuel. Water and land and air pollution. From animals raised to be eaten. Gone. Earth would heal. Her dying oceans recover. Animals would thrive. Without horrible suffering caused. By humans. No need to cut down rainforests. Any more. They could regenerate. And soak up more CO_2. Cooling the planet. No need to cut them down. For intensive factory farming. Of beef cattle. And crops to feed them. Humans would feel oh*so*good. Peaceful. Sort of spiritual. (Like I do. Chewing Brussels sprouts! On a summer's day.) About doing the right and mindful thing. Eating whole-foods plant-based diets. Kindness toward all beings. All life. Compassion spreading far and wide. If humans stopped. Breeding and killing animals. For food. And all the other stuff I told you about. They'd feel happy. A kind of wag-*wag*wagish joy! All life on Earth would feel relief.

And a dog eating a vegetable garden. Wouldn't be an ODDITY. Anymore. *Nosiree*! *Prance prance*. And laugh. *Phisst*!

Afterword

If a man aspires towards a righteous life, his first act of abstinence is from injury to animals.
—Albert Einstein

Gracie died. Two days before Christmas. A tumor had grown. Into her VENA CAVA. And she began to bleed out. Kathryn*the*veterinarian said she had a rare form. Of CUSHINGS DISEASE. Also common to Boxers. Grace's drool turned red. Jack washed her face. Fed her. By hand. No one could save her. Meg tried. So very hard. Drove Grace six hours. Each way. For treatments. I miss my friend. Really *really* miss her. We'd become sisters. Making up for the ones we lost.

By the end her skin was tissue paper thin. And the fur. On her back and sides. Had fallen out. She seemed tired. Wore a jacket for warmth.

During Gracie's last hours. At home. Spike lay next to his sibling. Rested his paw. On hers. Sam sat on the floor. And hugged her. Rubbed her ears. Ellie as well. I licked and licked Gracie's face. With all my love. Wanting to relieve her. Of misery. Then the time came. For Meg and Jack to lead Grace Elizabeth outside. She peed. Her custom. Just before a ride. They lifted her. Into the car. Close to midnight. And drove her away. She sat and looked out the back window. As she'd always done. One last time.

Ellie bought a house. For her and two cats. Nearby. And adopted a race horse. Sam moved. Into an apartment. His dad and step mother kicked him out. He'd smoked pot. In their home! Ooph! (Since then, Laws have changed. Not a big deal. Anymore.) And Perle Oonagh came to live with us. Rescued in Alabama just before they put her. And her nine unborn puppies. Into a gas chamber. She got to keep *her* tail! She's white. Too. We look alike. A little bit.

Perle attacked me. Again and again. So I fought her. Kathryn*the*veterinarian stitched us up. Now I have scars. On my face and ears. And legs. So does Perle. On walks she would scream and thrash. At the end of her leash. Whenever she saw her kind. During one BOUT. She slipped her harness. Attacked a neighbor's dog. The police came. To our house! Ooph! Ooph! Ooph!

Five trainers gave up. On us. We fought more. And fought. More than once. Meg pried our jaws open. Blood everywhere. Perle broke through a glass door. Coming for *me*! Meg telephoned behaviorists. Around the country. Every one said, "Once females fight, they can *never* live together." They warned Meg and Jack, "Perle cannot be near other dogs. Re-home her as an only dog or put her down!" Ooph!

So Meg took a pretty picture. Of Perle. For posters. That she hung. In the food co-op. And at the Unitarian Church. Meg cried. Every day. For months. Dreading her loss. But nobody wanted Perle. Well one woman did. Until Perle *peed* on her!

Only choice. Do what others said couldn't be done. Lucky for me and Perle. Those two were determined. Meg and Jack worked. With us. Daily. For hours. Doubled down. For three years. They taught us not to be afraid. Of one another. How to play together. How to trust and share. A Harvard psychologist told Meg. That she and Jack re-wired our brains! *Yessiree*!! Without even using colanders. On our heads. With lots of colorful wires. Sticking out. Nope! No need for brain-scanning Keymaster colander helmets. Not with Meg and Jack in charge!

These days we romp and play. Best friends. Perle and I walk. Ever so nicely. Side by side. I wash her face and ears. Calms her. Like when my mom licked me. We sleep back to back. On the bed. Sometimes she rests her head. On my neck. The way my sister Pepper and I slept.

Safe. While Jack and Meg read. And watch movies. At night. With Spike in the mix. Too. Though once in a great while. Perle and I almost have a KERFUFFLE. Almost.

We moved at last. To the big old *fixed*up house. In New Hampshire. Not too far. From Bob's and Nancy's place. In Vermont. Sophie died. Soon after we arrived. Then Maggie died. Snug against Jack's chest. Peaceful. In his arms. Spike's deaf. Now. And wobbly. Too wobbly to carry his clean bedding. Upstairs. From the laundry. Anymore.

Meg and Jack left our *flower*chair behind. But we have another. That's mid-century modern. Um hm! I sleep in the new chair. Share it. With Perle. We take turns. No more nights in my crate. They left behind the big kitchen table. As well. The one Gracie and I used to hide under. When Meg went all screechy. She doesn't call me "Damn*you*Dori." Anymore. Nope! Kind of rethought how humans frighten dogs. She wonders what it's like to be controlled. By members. Of the most predatory. And destructive species. On Earth. Yup! The woman's toned down. Cooled off.

Not the planet though. Heating up. Faster and faster. Every day more bad news. Millions. Of climate refugees. And over one billion by 2050. On the move. Now wildfires burn *inside* the Arctic Circle. Millions more acres burned up. In our country. Last year. And only two of 18,000 baby penguins survived. In an Antarctic colony. The rest starved. Because of Global Warming. And industrial-scale fishing. And our past president. Who eats dead mothers. Um hm. *Ground*up dairy cows! From McDonalds. And who likes to grab women's cats. Pulled our country out. Of the Paris Climate Agreement. And destroyed every piece. Of environmental protection legislation he could. Right and left. Said Global Warming and Climate Change are *fake* news! But not the United Nations. In 2018 it issued a new report. Now humans have only nine years to reduce greenhouse gases. By forty-five percent. If they want to survive. Nine years! Less than one dog's lifetime! Meg says, "We're *cooked*!" And U. S. women no longer have the right to control their bodies. Just like dogs never have. And farmed animals. And research and zoo and circus animals. Then there's COVID. Everywhere. And more to come. The Arctic is heating up four times faster. Than the global average. Ooph! Ooph! Ooph! Anyhoo I like cats! Too.

The good news. Jack and Meg still grow vegetable gardens! The CEO of Tyson foods announced "the future will be meatless." *Phisst!* Let's hope! Cross my paws. Nancy now serves vegan haggis. Slowly around the world. More and more rivers and the Ojibwe wild rice have had their fULL LEGAL RIGHTS recognized. Too. And the Himalayan Glaciers. All given rights to exist. By humans who took them away. And the brood of three robin chicks. Who nested on the ladder. By the porch door. FLEDGED. Flufl flufl flufl. To the big maple. And beyond. Wagwagwag!

Resources

In their behavior towards creatures, all men are Nazis. The smugness with which man can do with other species as he pleases exemplifies the most extreme racist theories, the principle that might is right.
—Isaac Bashevis Singer—author and Holocaust survivor

Let me say it openly: we are surrounded by an enterprise of degradation, cruelty, and killing which rivals anything the Third Reich was capable of, indeed dwarfs it, in that our is an enterprise without end, self-regenerating, bringing rabbits, rats, poultry, livestock, water animals ceaselessly into the world for the purpose of killing them.
—J. M. Coetzee—(author of *The Lives of Animals*)

— Books —

An Unnatural Order —Jim Mason
Beasts —Jeffrey Moussaieff Masson
Beyond Words— What Animals Think and Feel —Carl Safina
Dominion —Matthew Scully
Eaarth —Bill McKibben
Eat Like You Care —Gary Francione
Entangled Empathy —Lori Gruen
Eternal Treblinka: Our Treatment of Animals and the Holocaust
    —Charles Patterson

How Not to Die —Dr. Michael Greger

Hot —Mark Hertsgaard

Plant Strong —Rip Esselstn

Sistah Vegan —Edited by Dr. Amie Breeze Harper, Editor

Sister Species —Edited by Lisa Kemmerer

The China Study —Dr. T. Colin Campbell

The Dreaded Comparison: Human and Animal Slavery
    —Marjorie Spiegel

The Emotional Lives of Animals —Marc Bekoff

The Pig Who Sang to the Moon —Jeffrey Mousaieff Masson

The Pornography of Meat — Carol Adams

The Sexual Politics of Meat —Carol Adams

The Twenty-one Day Kickstart Diet —Dr. Neal Barnard

What a Fish Knows —Jonathan Balcombe

World Peace Diet —Dr. Will Tuttle

Why We Love Dogs, Eat Pigs and Wear Cows —Dr. Melanie Joy

— Documentaries & Films —

The assumption that animals are without rights, and the illusion that our treatment of them has no moral significance, is a positively outrageous example of Western crudity and barbarity. Universal compassion is the only guarantee of morality. Compassion for animals is intimately associated with goodness of character, and it may be confidently asserted that he who is cruel to animals cannot be a good man.
    —Arthur Schopenhauer

Of all the animals, man is the only one that is cruel. He is the only one who inflicts pain for the pleasure of doing it. It is a trait that is unknown to the higher animals.
    —Mark Twain

Babe
Charlotte's Web
Cowspiracy
Dominion
Earthlings
Eating You Alive
Forks over Knives
Lucent
Okja
Peaceable Kingdom
The Ghosts in the Machine
Racing Extinction
Seaspiracy
The Cove
The Game Changers
The Last Pig
The Witness
Unlocking the Cage
Vegan Everyday Stories
Vegucated
What the Health

— Recipes —

Veganism is a moral and ethical way of living in the world. It is the practice of non-cooperation and non-participation in anything that exploits nonhuman animals, humans, and the environment. It is a moral baseline for our conduct and how we are revealed to the world.
—Animal Rights of Rochester
(formerly Animal Rights of Upstate New York)

Isa Does It —Isa Chandra Moskowitz
The Wicked Healthy Cookbook —Chad Sarno, Derek Sarno, David Joachim
Vegan Eats World —Terry Hope Romero
Vegan in 7 —Rita Serano
Veganomicon —Isa Chandra Moskowitz
Vegan Yum Yum —Lauren Ulm

— Organizations —

When we think about farm animals, it is important to keep in mind that the purpose of their existence is almost entirely defined by their death and exploitation. We breed them to kill them and to profit from them—not to provide them with a way of fulfilling their destiny for a happy life. No amount of philosophical blather can get us past this immovable rock of, may we call it human treachery.
—Jeffrey Masson—author The Pig Who Sang to the Moon

Animal Kill Clock
Dawn Watch
Faunalytics
Humane Myth
In Defense of Animals
Lady Freethinker
Mercy for Animals
Moms Against Milk
PETA
Physicians Committee for Responsible Medicine
Switch4Good
The Vegan Society (vegansociety.com)
Vegan Action (vegan.org)

— Magazines —

For man is the cruelest animal. At tragedies, bull-fights, and crucifixions hath he hitherto been happiest on earth; and when he invented his hell, behold, that was his heaven on earth.
—Friedrich Nietzsche

The Vegan Magazine
Vegan Food and Living
Vegan Health and Fitness Magazine
Vegan Life
VegNews

— Farmed Animal Sanctuaries —

We are all victims of the violence animals suffer … their liberation is also our liberation.
—George Bernard Shaw

Farm Sanctuary —Watkins Glen, NY
Rancho Compasión —Nicasio, CA
Rowdy Girl Sanctuary —Angleton, TX
VINE Sanctuary —Springfield, VT

Acknowledgements

First and foremost, my deep gratitude goes to Michael Mirolla, Guernica Editions editor in chief, for accepting my manuscript. After that, his patience was legendary. He knew the best way to move my book forward was to step back as I revised and revised—a kind and restrained expression of faith in me, which he seasoned with his waggish sense of humor!

Before the manuscript found its way to Guernica Editions, many generous and wise people read this cross-genre story. Raw early versions. Evolving drafts. Their remarks helped us refine the ideas and words on these pages. The honest critiques bit a bit. But we took them to heart. The writing improved in leaps and bounds after each reader responded. And I, Dori, became more outspoken. In the process. That happens when a dog discovers her real voice. Has the chance to speak truth to power.

As for our readers, Jack Hurley has been the constant. Years of re-reading. Always kind. Insightful. Patient and witty. But blunt. Janet Siegel—the other long-term reader, who went over the manuscript from the first few pages through the next-to-last draft—brought her knowledge of environmental science, the vegan ethic, feminism, and teaching to the task. She, too, has been uplifting. Constructive. And forthright!

One writer and activist, who supported with enthusiasm this book early on, was Dr. Will Tuttle. His best-seller *The World Peace Diet* had informed Meg's and Jack's transition to the vegan ethic. Filmmaker and script writer Nora Jacobson read an early draft, as well, and her astute suggestions have held. Poet William Heyen read a later take, and his warm reaction reassured us that we were on the right track. Poet and editor Carol Westberg pored over the more evolved work, and offered solid ideas for revisions. Animal-rights activists Dawn Bradshaw, Ann Smith, and BJ Wahl added encouragement to the mix. Poet and artist Rob Plath read a late draft, and his excited email told us that all the hard work and innovation had been well worth the struggle.

A priceless contribution to the book came from Dr. A. Breeze Harper. An intersectional writer and thorough, compassionate critic, she analyzed the text through different, yet essential lenses and sensitivities, and questioned historical, social, and ethical stands in the writing, bringing the work to its deepest level as commentary from the perspectives of the justice movements: women's, civil rights, LGBTQIA+, environmental, and animal rights.

Joni B. Cole, author and founder of the Writer's Center in White River Junction, Vermont, worked with Meg, re-envisioning the query letter. She made a daring prediction, that the manuscript would have a publisher within three weeks of sending out the revised query, which brought in more and faster responses—and much interest. The book's realization seemed to shift from *possible* to *probable*. Then our story found its home at Guernica Editions. Joni was off by four days!

Luck led us to Minneapolis painter and vegan Mary Bergherr, cover artist. She lives the ethic central to our story, and creates saucy and irreverent messaged art. A perfect match for our book.

Each reader's contributions and kindness kept us afloat through rewrites and submissions. And fill us with gratitude. As do all the activists and writers whose works on animal rights and sentience helped us grow closer to animals. We could not have written this book without them.

Dori and Meg Hurley
Claremont, NH

About the Authors

Writer. Abolitionist animal-rights activist. Feminist. Sometimes a painter. Adoptive mother of two Korean-born grown children. Meg Hurley's writing focuses on animal and women's rights and international adoption. Her work has been published in magazines, newspapers, and anthologies in the United States and Korea, including *Ms.*, *Mothering*, *Parents*, *Gokdongsanae*, and *Yosong Shinmun*. Recognized in *Best American Essays* as a Notable Essayist, she was also nominated by former Grove Atlantic editor Alison Draper for the Pushcart Editor's Book Award "for books rejected by today's bottom line, profit driven commercial presses." In 1995, Meg was the first Westerner to interview Korean birthmothers. The film *The Hanji Box* (Amazon Prime) is based on her experiences in Korea. Up next, revising her collection of poems for publication. All vegan, Meg and her husband and dogs live in New Hampshire. She is a graduate of Wellesley College.

Best friend. Alter ego. Willful. Independent. Mouthy. Dorothea Orane Hurley keeps her human family in line, making them question and assess their relationships with animals. Raw yams, cooked broccoli, blueberry Clif Bars, baked tofu, barbequed tempeh, nutritional yeast, and coconut yogurt are some of Dori's favorite foods. Sniffing and snoozing are her pastimes. She hasn't ransacked anymore vegetable gardens. Every day, she and Perle and their humans go on long walks, unless the weather is unbearable. No more chasing squirrels. This is her first book. For more information, visit Dori's website: www.vegdogsavesplanet.com